EMIL'S CLEVER PIG

ASTRID LINDGREN

EMIL'S CLEVER PIG

Illustrated by Tony Ross

OXFORD
UNIVERSITY PRESS

OXFORD
UNIVERSITY PRESS

Great Clarendon Street, Oxford OX2 6DP

Oxford University Press is a department of the University of Oxford.
It furthers the University's objective of excellence in research, scholarship,
and education by publishing worldwide in

Oxford   New York

Auckland   Cape Town   Dar es Salaam   Hong Kong   Karachi
Kuala Lumpur   Madrid   Melbourne   Mexico City   Nairobi
New Delhi   Shanghai   Taipei   Toronto

With offices in

Argentina   Austria   Brazil   Chile   Czech Republic   France   Greece
Guatemala   Hungary   Italy   Japan   Poland   Portugal   Singapore
South Korea   Switzerland   Thailand   Turkey   Ukraine   Vietnam

Oxford is a registered trade mark of Oxford University Press
in the UK and in certain other countries

Database right Oxford University Press (maker)

First published as Än lever Emil i Lönneberga, Rabén & Sjögren, Stockholm 1970
First published in English 1973 by Brockhampton Press Ltd
First published in this edition 2008 by Oxford University Press

This translation of Emil's Clever Pig originally published in Swedish
published by arrangement with Saltkråkan Förvaltning AB

British Library Cataloguing in Publication Data

Data available

ISBN: 978-0-19-272756-5

7 9 10 8

Printed in Great Britain

Paper used in the production of this book is a natural, recyclable product
made from wood grown in sustainable forests. The manufacturing process
conforms to the environmental regulations of the country of origin.

Contents

There was never a boy in the whole of Lönneberga and in the whole of Småland and in the whole of Sweden and—who knows—perhaps in the whole world who got into more mischief than Emil. He lived at Katthult farm in Lönneberga in Småland in Sweden a long time ago. No one would have believed that when he grew up he would become the president of the local council and the finest man in the whole of Lönneberga, but he did.

Alma Svensson of Katthult, who was Emil's mother, wrote down all his tricks in blue exercise books, which she kept in a drawer in her desk. Eventually, the drawer was so jammed with exercise books that it was almost impossible to open it, because one book always curled up and got stuck. But those exercise books are all there in the same old desk today, except for the three that Emil once tried to sell to his Sunday School teacher when he was in need of money. She didn't want to buy them; so he made paper boats out of them and sailed the boats in the stream at Katthult, and no one has ever seen those three books since.

The Sunday School teacher did not understand why she was expected to buy Emil's exercise books.

'What would I do with them?' she asked in surprise.

'Teach the children not to be as naughty as me,' said Emil.

Oh yes, Emil knew perfectly well what a naughty boy he was, and if he ever managed to forget it, there was always Lina, the maidservant at Katthult, to remind him.

'It's a waste of time for you to go to Sunday School,' she said. 'It doesn't do you any good, and you'll never go to heaven anyway—well, unless they need you up there to help make thunder and lightning.'

'I've never seen anyone like that boy,' Lina said, shaking her head as she went off with little Ida, Emil's sister, to the meadow where little Ida could pick wild strawberries while Lina milked the cows. Ida threaded strawberries on a straw and came home with five straws full, and Emil only persuaded her to give him two straws, which shows that he wasn't so bad after all.

You mustn't think that Emil had wanted to go to the cow pasture with Lina and Ida. Oh no, he felt like doing something more exciting. So he grabbed his cap and his gun, and ran straight to the field and jumped on to Lukas, who then galloped off among the hazel bushes, making the clods fly up behind him. Emil was playing 'Småland's hussars attack'. He had seen a picture of the soldiers in the newspaper, so he knew just what they did.

His cap, his gun, and Lukas were Emil's dearest treasures. Lukas was his horse, yes, his very own horse, won through his cleverness at Vimmerby Fair. The cap was an ugly little blue peaked one that his father had bought for him. The gun was a wooden one, and Alfred, the farmhand at Katthult, had made it for Emil because he was very fond of him. Emil could easily have carved his own gun, for if anyone was good at carving it was Emil, but then he had plenty of practice. You see, every time Emil got into mischief he was punished by being sent to the tool shed, and there he would always carve a funny little wooden man. He had 369 wooden men, which are all there today, except for the one which his mother buried behind the red-currant bushes because it looked so like the parson.

'We can't let anyone see that,' Emil's mother had said.

Well, now you know something about Emil. You know that he played pranks all year round, summer and winter, and since I have read all of the blue exercise books, I'm going to tell you about some of the days in Emil's life. You will soon see that Emil did lots of nice things, too, so of course I shall tell you all about them as well as all about his terrible tricks. Some were worse than others and some were quite harmless. It was only on November 13 that he did something really outrageous. No, don't ask me to tell you about that. I'm never going to tell anyone because I promised Emil's mother. No, we'll take one of the days when Emil behaved fairly well on the whole, even though his father didn't think so.

*Saturday, the twelfth of June, when Emil bought
some useless junk at the auction at Backhorva which
turned out useful in the end.*

One Saturday in June there was an auction at Backhorva that everyone planned to attend, for auctions were what they enjoyed most in Lönneberga, and the whole of Småland. Emil's father, Anton Svensson, was going, of course. Alfred and Lina had pestered him so much that he had agreed to take them along too, and naturally Emil was going.

If you have ever been to an auction, you'll know what it is all about. You'll know that when people want to sell their belongings, they put them up for auction so that other people can bid on them and buy them. The people from Backhorva farm wanted to sell everything they had, for they were emigrating to America, as so many people did in those days, and they couldn't take their kitchen beds and frying pans and cows and pigs and hens with them. So, on this early summer day, there was going to be an auction at Backhorva.

Emil's father was hoping to get a bargain on a cow and perhaps a sow and possibly a couple of hens. That was why he was going to Backhorva and that was why he let Alfred and Lina go with him, for he would need their help to bring the animals home.

'But what Emil thinks he's going to do there, I don't know,' said Emil's father.

'We don't need Emil to make trouble,' said Lina, 'there's sure to be plenty of that anyway.'

Lina knew there usually were a lot of quarrels and fights at auctions in Lönneberga and all of Småland, so she was right in a way. But Emil's mother looked at her sternly and said, 'If Emil wants to go, he shall go. It's nothing to do with you. You just watch how you behave and don't go making eyes at the fellows like you usually do.'

That remark caused Lina to be quiet.

Emil put on his cap and was ready.

'Buy something for me,' said little Ida, as she tilted her head to one side.

She didn't say it to anyone in particular, but her father scowled.

'Buy, buy, buy, I never hear anything else. Didn't I buy you ten öre's worth of sugar-candy the other day—for your birthday in January, don't you remember?'

Emil was about to ask his father for some money, for you can't go to an auction with empty pockets, but then he thought he'd better not. It obviously wasn't the right moment to try to get money from his father, who was already sitting in the big milk cart, impatient to be off.

'What you can't get one way, you must get another,' Emil said to himself. He thought hard for a moment, and then he said, 'You go on ahead. I'll come later on Lukas.'

Emil's father was suspicious when he heard this, but he was anxious to be off as quickly as possible, and so he only said, 'All right, but it would be better if you stayed at home altogether.'

Then he cracked his whip and away they went. Alfred waved to Emil and Lina waved to little Ida, and Emil's mother shouted to Emil's father, 'See that you come home without any bones broken.'

She said that, because she also knew what terrible fights there sometimes were at auctions.

The milk cart disappeared rapidly round a bend in the road. Emil stood in the cloud of dust and watched them go. Then he got busy. He had to get money somehow, and you'll never guess how he did it.

If you had been a child in Småland when Emil was little, you would know all about the gates that were everywhere in those days. They were there to keep the cows and sheep of Småland in their pastures, and I think they were also there to help the Småland children earn a two öre piece each time they opened the gate for some farmer in his horse-drawn cart who was too lazy to open it himself.

Katthult had a gate too, but Emil had earned only a few precious two öre pieces from it, because Katthult was on the outskirts of the village and hardly anyone came that way. There was only one farm further away and that was Backhorva, the farm where the auction was to be held.

Which means that every man will have to come through our gate on his way to the auction, thought Emil, the clever boy.

Emil stood guard at the gate for a whole hour and he earned five kronor, seventy-four öre. Just imagine that! Horses and carts came in such a constant flow that he could barely shut the gate after one went through before he had to open it again for another. All the farmers passing through were in a good mood, because they were going to the auction, and cheerfully threw two and five öre pieces into Emil's cap. Some of the old fellows were so full of the joys of spring that they gave him a whole ten öre piece, though they probably regretted it immediately afterwards.

But the farmer from Kråkstorp went into a tantrum when Emil shut the gate in his brown mare's face.

'Why have you shut the gate?' he yelled.

'I've got to shut it first, before I can open it,' Emil explained.

'Why don't you leave it open on a day like this?' demanded the farmer, crossly.

'I'm not dumb,' said Emil. 'This is the first time I'm getting something out of this silly old gate.'

But the farmer from Kråkstorp flicked Emil with his whip and didn't give him a coin.

When everyone who was going to the auction had passed through Emil's gate and there was no more money to earn, Emil mounted Lukas and rode off so fast that the coins in his trouser pocket bounced and jingled.

The auction at Backhorva was now in full swing. People crowded round the items which had been taken out into the farmyard, where they looked very out of place in the bright sunlight. The auctioneer stood on a barrel in the centre of the hubbub, and the bidding was brisk for frying pans and coffee cups and old Windsor chairs and I don't know what else.

I'd better explain that at an auction you shout out to the auctioneer how much you want to pay for the item he is selling, but if there is anyone who is willing to pay more or bid higher, then he gets the kitchen bed or whatever it is.

A sort of sigh went through the crowd when Emil and Lukas came clattering into the farmyard, and you could hear some of them muttering, 'Here comes the Katthult boy; we might as well go home!'

Emil was anxious to start bargaining; since he had so much money in his pocket, he was quite dizzy with excitement. Even before he dismounted, he had bid three kronor for an old iron bedstead which he wouldn't ordinarily have wanted even if it had

15

been given to him. Fortunately, a farmer's wife bid four kronor for it, so Emil was saved. But he went on bidding enthusiastically for just about everything and in a flash he became the owner of three items. The first was a faded velvet-covered box with tiny blue shells on the lid which he planned to give to little Ida; the second was a bread shovel, one of those with a long handle for shoving the loaves into the bread oven; the third was a rusty old fire pump which no one in the whole of Lönneberga would have given even ten öre for. But Emil bid twenty-five and got it.

Oh help, I didn't want that, thought Emil. But it was too late now, he had a fire pump and that was that.

Alfred came and looked at Emil's pump and laughed.

'Fire pump owner Emil Svensson,' he said. 'What do you want that contraption for?'

'In case lightning strikes and starts a fire,' said Emil. And the next second lightning did strike, at

least that's what Emil thought, but it was only his father grabbing him by the collar and shaking him until his curly hair swayed.

'Wretched child. What do you think you're doing?' shouted Emil's father.

He had quietly been walking about through the cow pasture, picking out a cow for himself, when Lina had come running up quite out of breath, 'Master, Master, Emil's here and he's buying fire pumps for all he's worth. Is that all right?'

Emil's father did not know that Emil had any money of his own. He was sure that he would have to pay for anything which had been auctioned off to Emil, so you see it wasn't surprising that he went pale and quivered with fear when he heard about the fire pump.

'Let me go. I'm going to pay,' yelped Emil. Gradually he got a chance to explain how he had become so rich simply by opening the gate at Katthult. Emil's father admitted that it was rather smart of him, but said it wasn't at all smart to throw his money away again on an old fire pump.

'Don't let me hear that you've bid for any more idiotic bargains,' he said sternly.

He wanted to see everything that had been auctioned off to Emil and it was an awful shock when he did see them. The old velvet-covered box and the bread shovel were two absolutely useless bargains, but worst of all was the fire pump.

'Now remember what I've told you. You only buy things that are really necessary,' said Emil's father.

Maybe he was right, but how are you to know what is really necessary? Soda pop, for example, is that really necessary? Emil thought so anyway. He wandered round rather aimlessly after the talking-to his father had given him, and then in a lilac grove he spied a booth that sold beer and soda pop. The Backhorva family had always been rather enterprising, and they had brought home several crates from the brewery at Vimmerby to sell to all the thirsty people at the auction.

Emil had only drunk soda pop once in his life and his spirits soared when he suddenly realized that there was soda pop for sale and there was money in his pocket. What a lucky coincidence!

Emil had ordered and drunk three bottles of soda pop in rapid succession when the lightning struck again. His father suddenly reappeared and shook him so hard that the soda pop went up his nose.

'Wretched boy. So you stand there guzzling soda pop just because you've made a little money for once!'

Then Emil got really furious and he said so in quite plain terms.

'Now I'm mad. When I haven't any money, I *can't* drink soda pop. When I have got some money, I'm *not allowed* to drink soda pop. So when the heck *can* I drink soda pop?'

Emil's father looked at him sternly.

'This means the tool shed when you get home.'

He didn't say any more, but went back to look at the cows. Emil felt ashamed of himself. He realized how horrid he had been. Not only had he been rude to his father, but worst of all he had said 'heck', which was almost a swear word, and swear words were simply not allowed at Katthult. Emil's father was a churchwarden, you see.

He stood there ashamed for several minutes, then he bought another bottle of soda pop which he took to Alfred as a present. They sat down with their backs against the wall of the woodshed and talked while Alfred drank his soda pop—he'd never tasted anything so good in all his life, he said.

'Have you seen Lina?' asked Emil. Alfred pointed with his thumb to show Emil where she was. Lina was sitting in the grass with her back to a fence and beside her sat the farmer from Kråkstorp, the one who had flicked Emil with his whip. It was obvious that she had forgotten all about Emil's mother's warning, for she was flirting and laughing as she always did when she was out somewhere.

It was obvious that the Kråkstorp farmer liked Lina's flirting, and Emil was delighted to see it.

'Just think, Alfred, if we could marry her off to the Kråkstorp farmer,' he said hopefully, 'then she'd stop running after you.'

You see Lina had decided on Alfred as her fiancé, and she had made up her mind to marry him, although Alfred tried his best to put her off.

The problem of saving Alfred from Lina had worried both Alfred and Emil for a long time now; they cheered up at the thought of the Kråkstorp farmer taking a fancy to her. He was old, of course, and quite bald, but he had a little farm of his own and it would surely please Lina to be the wife of the Kråkstorp farmer.

'We must take care that no one disturbs them,' said Emil.

He knew Lina would have to flatter and flirt a lot before the Kråkstorp farmer would lose his common sense and swallow the bait!

Emil's father managed to buy a sow that was going to have piglets, but there was a lot of bidding for the cows. A farmer from Bastefall wanted all seven of them, and Emil's father had to bid eighty kronor to get the cow that he wanted. He groaned as he paid out such an awful sum, for now he had no money left to buy any hens. The man from Bastefall bid for them and got them, all except one, which he didn't want.

'What good's a lame hen to me? You'd better wring her neck!'

The hen the Bastefall farmer didn't want had broken her leg once and it had healed at a funny angle—that was why the poor creature limped so badly.

But one of the boys from Backhorva farm was standing next to Emil and said to him, 'What a stupid old man not to want Lame Lotta, she's our best layer, you know.'

Then Emil shouted loudly, 'I bid twenty-five öre for Lame Lotta.'

Everyone laughed, everyone except Emil's father. He came rushing up and seized Emil by the collar.

'Wretched child. How many more idiotic bargains are you going to make today? This means double time in the tool shed.'

But what was done was done. Emil had bid twenty-five öre, and that was the end of it. Lame Lotta was his, whether his father liked it or not.

'Anyway, now I have two animals of my own, a horse and a hen,' he said to Alfred.

'Yes, a horse and a lame hen.' Alfred laughed, but in a nice way.

Lame Lotta was given to Emil in a box and he put her with his other treasures over by the woodshed. His fire pump and his bread shovel and his velvet-covered box were all there, and Lukas was tied up beside them. Emil looked at his properly and felt rather pleased.

But how was Lina getting on with her farmer in the meantime?

Emil and Alfred went off to see and noticed with

satisfaction that she was doing very well for herself. The farmer had his arm round her waist, and Lina was squiggling and giggling harder than ever. Every once in a while she pushed him away so that he rolled over backwards against the fence.

'He seems to like her all right,' said Emil, 'let's hope she doesn't push too hard.'

Emil and Alfred were very satisfied with Lina's behaviour, but someone else was not, and he was Bulten i Bo. Bulten i Bo was the worst ruffian and carouser in the whole of Lönneberga; it was nearly always his fault that there were so many wild fights at auctions, because he was the one who began them.

Now you must understand that in those days a farm lad worked and slaved week after week all the year round and hardly ever got away from his farm, so you see an auction like this was a chance to enjoy himself. What he liked most was to have a good fight. He didn't know what else to do with all that wild energy which suddenly bubbled up inside him when there were lots of people about and he had had a couple of strong drinks—for not everyone stuck to soda pop, not Bulten i Bo anyway.

As he was going by, he saw Lina flirting with the Kråkstorp farmer and said, 'Aren't you ashamed of yourself, Lina? What are you doing with a bald-headed old buffer like that? He's much too old for you.'

That's how fights begin.

Emil and Alfred stood and watched the anger rising up in the Kråkstorp farmer as he let go of Lina. Why should Bulten i Bo have to come along right now and spoil Alfred's and Emil's plans!

'No, stay where you are,' shouted Emil anxiously to the Kråkstorp farmer. 'I'll take care of Bulten.'

He picked up the bread shovel and hit Bulten firmly on the backside with it. That was a mistake, for Bulten turned round, purple with rage, and grabbed Emil, who found himself dangling from two enormous hands and wondering if his last moment had come.

But then Alfred shouted, 'Leave the boy alone or, sure as I'm alive, I'll bash you to smithereens.'

Alfred was strong too, and all set for a fight, so in less than two seconds he and Bulten were at it hammer and tongs.

This was what everyone had been waiting for.

Several farm lads had already been wondering when a fight was going to start, and now they came running up from all sides to join in.

'They're fighting over me,' shrieked Lina. 'What a drama!'

'There'll be no drama here so long as I've got my bread shovel,' said Emil, confidently.

By now all the farm lads were rolling about on the ground in one great heap. They pulled and tore and bit and thumped and pounded each other, and yelled like troopers. And right at the bottom of the heap were Alfred and Bulten and the farmer from Kråkstorp. Emil was afraid they might finish off his Alfred altogether, and he poked about in the heap with his bread shovel, rather as if he were playing spillikins, trying to help Alfred get out. But he didn't succeed because wherever he poked, an angry hand always stuck out and tried to drag him down into the fight.

Emil didn't fancy that, so he jumped up on to Lukas and galloped round and round the battle. With his hair flying and bread shovel ready, he passed by on his horse, and he looked like a knight charging into the battle with lance poised. As he rode round, he started bashing anyone within reach with his bread shovel. He got a much better swing on horseback and actually succeeded in peeling off the topmost layer of farm lads, but more and more kept rushing up and hurling themselves on to the heap. No matter how hard he worked with his bread shovel, he couldn't get Alfred out.

Now all the women and children had started the most fearful sobbing and screaming, and Emil's father and the other sensible farmers, who were too proud to fight, merely stood by and said helplessly, 'That's enough now, boys, there'll be lots more auctions, so save a little blood for them.'

But the farm lads were so busy that they didn't hear anything. All they wanted to do was fight and fight and go on fighting.

Emil threw down his bread shovel.

'Now, Lina, you must help and not just stand there screaming,' he said. 'Don't forget, it's your fiancé at the bottom of that lot.'

I've told you before that Emil was a smart boy, and guess what he did. He took his fire pump and filled it with water from the nearby stream. He made

Lina pump and he aimed the hose, and you should have seen the water shooting out!

It was as if the pile of lads hiccuped when the first jet of ice-cold water hit them full force. Believe me, Emil only had to squirt them for a couple of minutes before the fight slowed down and came to a halt. One farm lad after another stuck an astonished swollen face out of the pile and slowly got to his feet.

If you ever come across a fight and you want to stop it, don't forget that cold water is better than a bread shovel any day.

The farm lads weren't at all angry. Now that they had got rid of all their pent-up energies, they were quite glad that the fight was over for today.

'Anyway, there's an auction at Knashult next week,' said Bulten i Bo, as he held a handful of moss under his nose until the bleeding stopped.

Then Emil went to the Knashult farmer, who was there, too, and had seen the fight, and sold him the fire pump for fifty öre.

'I made twenty-five öre on that deal,' said Emil to Alfred.

And it was on June 12 at Backhorva when Alfred realized that Emil might easily become an important businessman when he grew up.

The auction was over now and everyone was preparing to go home. The sow was loaded into the milk cart and Lame Lotta was allowed to travel there, too, although Emil's father glared at her sitting quietly in her box. It was decided that Rölla, the cow, should plod along behind, but no one had asked her what she thought about such an arrangement.

Perhaps you've heard about angry bulls, but do you know about wild cows? If you don't, I can tell you that when a cow gets really wild, the other animals tremble at the knees and even the fiercest of them run away and hide.

Rölla had always been the gentlest and best-behaved cow you could imagine, but when Alfred and Lina tried to drive her out on to the road to take her home with them, she kicked her hind legs high and ran off, giving such a hideous bellow that everyone at the auction was petrified. Perhaps she had seen the farm lads fighting and thought that was what you were supposed to do at an auction and wanted to join in, too. At any rate, she had gone stark-raving mad and it was impossible to get near her. Alfred tried first, and then Emil's father, but Rölla charged towards them with wild eyes flashing and lowered horns, bellowing furiously, and both Alfred and Emil's father had to run like hares to get away. Several others tried to help, but Rölla wasn't going to have anyone in her farmyard and she chased them all out.

'What a drama,' said Lina as she watched first the Backhorva farmer, then the Kråkstorp farmer, then the Knashult farmer, then the Bastefall farmer, and then Bulten i Bo run for their lives with Rölla at their heels.

Finally Emil's father began to rave, too, and shouted, 'Eighty kronor I've given for that infernal

cow and what she needs is shooting! Fetch a gun someone!'

He shuddered as he said it, but he knew that a mad cow was no use to anyone. Everyone else knew it, too; so the Backhorva farmer fetched his loaded gun and handed it to Emil's father.

'You'd better do it yourself,' he said.

But Emil shouted, 'Wait a minute.'

I've already told you that he was a smart boy. He went up to his father and said, 'If you're really going to shoot her, you might just as well give her to me.'

'What do you want a mad cow for,' asked Emil's father, 'to hunt lions with?'

But Emil's father knew that Emil was good with animals; so he said that if Emil could get Rölla home to Katthult, she would be Emil's cow for ever, stark-raving mad or not.

Then Emil went up to the Bastefall farmer, the one who had bought the other six cows, and said, 'How much will you pay me to drive your cows as far as Katthult?'

Bastefall farm was at the other end of the parish, and the Bastefall farmer knew it wasn't going to be any joke to drive six cows ahead of him all that way; so he promptly took a twenty-five öre piece out of his pocket.

'Go ahead,' he said. 'Take this.'

Guess what Emil did then. He ran right across the

farmyard past Rölla, into the cow house and untied the cows which were tied up there, and when he drove them towards Rölla, she stopped in the middle of a bellow and cast her eyes down, obviously ashamed of her bad behaviour. But what does a poor cow do

34

when forced to go away alone and leave her old farmyard and the other cows she has always been with? She gets frightened and upset, but only Emil had understood that.

Now Rölla trotted along, as nice as you please, with the other cows out into the road, and everyone at the auction laughed and said, 'The Katthult boy isn't so dumb after all.'

Alfred laughed too.

'Animal owner, Emil Svensson,' he said. 'Now you have a horse, a lame hen, and a mad cow. Are you sure you wouldn't like any more animals?'

'In time I shall certainly have more,' said Emil, calmly.

Emil's mother was standing at the kitchen window watching for her family's return, and her eyes nearly popped out of her head when she saw the stately procession coming along the road. First came the milk cart with Emil's father and Alfred and Lina and the sow and Lame Lotta, who was clucking excitedly over a newly laid egg. Then came *seven* cows in a long row and last of all, riding Lukas, Emil, who was keeping the cows neatly in line, with the bread shovel. Emil's mother rushed out with little Ida at her heels.

'*Seven* cows,' she shrieked at Emil's father. 'Who's gone crazy, you or me?'

'No, the cow,' mumbled Emil's father, but he had to mumble a more detailed explanation before Emil's mother understood everything that had happened at the auction. Then she looked fondly at Emil.

'Bless you, Emil. But however could you have guessed that only a few minutes ago my bread shovel broke in half when I was putting the loaves into the oven!'

But she shrieked again when she saw Alfred's nose, which was twice as big as usual.

'Where on earth did you get that nose?' she asked.

'At the Backhorva auction, and next Saturday I'm going to take it to another auction at Knashult.'

Lina climbed gloomily down from the milk cart. All her flirting and giggling were over.

'What a sour-looking face,' said Emil's mother. 'What's the matter with you?'

'Toothache,' Lina replied dully. The Kråkstorp farmer had offered her lots of sweets, which had given her such a bad toothache that her head felt ready to burst.

But toothache or not, she had to go straight out to the meadow to milk the Katthult cows, for it was long past milking time.

It was also long past milking time for Rölla and the other cows from the auction, and they mooed loudly to make sure everyone knew about it.

'Well, it's not my fault if the farmer from Bastefall isn't here to milk his own cows,' Emil said, and began milking them himself, first Rölla and then the other six cows.

So he got six gallons of milk, and his mother put it down in the cellar and made cheese out of it later. There was lots of cheese, enough for Emil and the others to eat for a lovely long time.

Emil boiled the egg straightaway, the one Lame Lotta had laid on the way home, and put it on the kitchen table in front of his father, who was waiting sullenly for his supper.

'That's from Lame Lotta,' said Emil.

Next he poured out a glass of fresh milk for his father.

'That's from Rölla,' he said.

His father ate and drank in silence while his mother pushed all the loaves of bread into the oven.

After milking the cows, Lina returned to the kitchen. She held a hot potato against her aching tooth, which made it ache seven times worse, as she knew it would.

'Now, see how you like that,' Lina said to the tooth. 'That's tit for tat.'

Alfred laughed.

'The Kråkstorp farmer was very nice to give you all those sweets wasn't he?' he said. 'He's the man you ought to marry, Lina!'

Lina snorted.

'That old goat. He's fifty years old, and I'm only twenty-five. Do you think I want someone twice as old as I am?'

'That's all right,' said Emil quickly. 'It doesn't make any difference.'

'Yes it does,' said Lina. 'It's all right now. But just think, when I'm fifty he'll be a hundred, and the Lord only knows the trouble I'll have with him then.'

'You reckon according to your lights,' said Emil's mother, and slammed the oven door on the last load of bread. 'That's a first-class bread shovel, Emil,' she added.

When Emil's father had eaten his egg and drunk

his milk, Emil said, 'Aren't I supposed to be going to the tool shed?'

Emil's father muttered something to the effect that when all was said and done Emil hadn't really done anything bad enough to sit in the tool shed for, but Emil said, 'No, no, you must keep your word.'

He went solemnly out to the tool shed and began to carve his one hundred and twenty-ninth wooden man.

By this time Lame Lotta was already sitting on her perch in the hen house, and Rölla was wandering about quite happily in the meadow with the Katthult cows. After a while the Bastefall farmer came to fetch his six cows. He and Emil's father had a good long chat about the auction and everything that had happened there, so it was quite a while before Emil's father could go to let Emil out, but as soon as the Bastefall farmer had gone he hurried to the tool shed.

As he came near, he saw little Ida perched on a

stool outside the tool-shed window. In her hands she had the velvet-covered box with the shells on it, and she was grasping it as if it was the finest thing she'd ever held, and indeed it was.

But Emil's father muttered, 'Crazy buy. An old velvet-covered box.'

She hadn't noticed her father coming, so she went on obediently repeating the words which Emil was whispering to her from inside the dark tool shed. Emil's father turned pale when he heard what she was saying, because he was a church-warden and more terrible words had never been uttered at Katthult. Just because Ida was saying them in her sweet little voice, it didn't make them any better.

'Silence, Ida,' roared Emil's father, as he put his hand through the window and grabbed Emil by the collar. 'Wretched child, have you been sitting there teaching your sister to swear?'

'No, I haven't,' said Emil. 'I've only been telling her that she must never say "heck", and I've been

teaching her lots of other words that she must never say.'

So now you know what Emil did on June 12. And even if not all of it was good, you must admit that he made some very shrewd deals. Now just count all those things he got on the very same day—a fine cow, a good laying hen, a bread shovel, and enough milk from the cows to make lots of cheese.

The only thing that his father could grumble about was the old velvet-covered box which wasn't actually worth anything, although little Ida loved it dearly. In it she put her scissors and her thimble and a little songbook she had won at Sunday School and a pretty piece of blue glass and her red hair ribbon. When she was given the box there was a bundle of old letters in it which she threw on the floor. But when Emil was let out of the tool shed and went into the kitchen on Saturday evening, he saw the packet of letters lying in a corner and picked it up. Alfred was walking round with a fly-swatter, swatting flies for dear life so that Lina would have no flies in her kitchen on Sunday. Emil showed him the packet of letters.

'You never know when these may come in handy,' said Emil. 'If I ever have to send anyone a letter, I've got a whole pile here already written.'

On top of the bundle lay a letter from America and Emil whistled when he saw it.

'Look, Alfred. We've got Adrian's letter here.'

Adrian was the eldest son of the Backhorva farmer.

He had gone to America a long time ago and in all that time had only written home once—everyone in Lönneberga knew that, and they were all disgusted with him, because they felt sorry for his poor parents. What he actually did write in the letter no one found out, since the people at Backhorva kept very quite about it.

'Now we can see what was in it,' Emil said, as he was a clever boy and had taught himself to read.

He opened the letter and read it aloud to Alfred. It didn't take long, as the letter was so short. This is what it said: 'I have seed a bear. Send yore adress. Goodbye for now.'

'It doesn't look as if that letter is going to be much use to me,' said Emil.

But it was.

Then the evening came. Saturday, June 12, was nearly over, night fell on Katthult with peace and quiet to all who lived there, humans as well as animals. All except Lina, who had a toothache.

She lay awake on her kitchen bed, moaning and groaning throughout the short June night and until a new day came.

A new day in Emil's life, too.

Sunday, the thirteenth of June, when Emil made three brave attempts to pull Lina's tooth and then painted little Ida blue.

Cows have to be milked, even on Sundays. At five o'clock in the morning the alarm clock went off in the kitchen and Lina staggered out of bed with the most terrible toothache. She took one look at herself in the mirror and gave a shrill scream. Good heavens, what a sight she was! Her right cheek was swollen up like a big breakfast bun. No, it was too awful. Lina began to cry.

It was a real shame, for this was the very day that nearly the whole village was coming to Katthult for an after-church coffee party.

'I can't possibly let them all see me with one side of my face different from the other,' moaned Lina, and she went off to milk the cows, sniffling.

She hadn't long to worry about one side being different from the other, for no sooner had she seated herself on the milking stool than a wasp came and stung her on the left cheek. You'd think she would have been happy now, for her left cheek swelled up at once and was just the same size as the other one. Now she had what she wanted, for she looked the same on both sides, but she cried harder than ever.

When she came into the kitchen, everyone was sitting at the breakfast table, and I can tell you that their eyes opened wide when the swollen-cheeked, red-eyed creature that was supposed to be Lina suddenly appeared in the doorway. Poor girl, the sight of her was enough to make anyone cry; so it wasn't very nice of Emil to laugh.

He was just going to drink some milk as Lina came in. When he caught sight of her over the top of his glass he snorted so hard that the milk flew right across the table and splattered all over his father's fine Sunday waistcoat. Then Alfred gave a little snigger, too. Emil's mother looked sternly at Emil and Alfred, and said that this was no laughing matter. But while she was wiping the milk off Emil's father's waistcoat, she took another look at Lina and she understood why Emil had snorted—although she really felt sorry for Lina.

'Poor girl,' she said. 'You look awful. You'll have to keep out of the way when the guests come. Emil, you'll have to run over to Krösa-Maja's and ask her to come and help us serve the coffee.'

The Lönneberga people like drinking after-church coffee on Sundays; so on the farms all round everyone had been delighted when a letter came from Emil's mother saying:

Dear Ladies and Gentlemen,

Alma and Anton Svensson of Katthult, Lönneberga, cordially invite you to an after-church coffee party on Sunday.

Now it was time to go to church. Emil's father and mother set off. Obviously they had to go to church first, before there could *be* any after-church coffee.

Emil went off obediently with the message to Krösa-Maja. It was a beautiful morning, and he was whistling gaily when he turned on to the path that led to her cabin in the forest.

If you have ever been in a forest in Småland on an early summer morning in June, you know just what it is like. You hear the cuckoo call and the blackbirds whistle, you feel the softness of the path strewn with pine needles under your bare feet and the warmth of the sun on your neck. You walk along smelling the resin from the fir trees and the pine trees, and in the glades you see the white blossoms of the wild strawberries. Emil was enjoying the walk so much that he took a long time to get to Krösa-Maja's, but at last he came to her cabin, which was so small and grey and ramshackle that you hardly noticed it among the pines.

Inside sat Krösa-Maja reading the *Småland's Daily News* and gloating over some horrifying story she had found in it.

'*Typhus* has come to Jönkoping,' she said, before she had even said good morning to Emil, and she pushed the newspaper under his nose so that he could read it himself. Sure enough, it stated that two inhabitants of Jönkoping were seriously ill with typhus, and Krösa-Maja nodded her head delightedly.

'Typhus is a horrible disease,' she said. 'And we'll soon have it here in Lönneberga, mark my words.'

'But why? How can it get here?' asked Emil.

'It's flying all over Småland like dandelion seeds, even while you're standing here,' said Krösa-Maja. 'Pounds and pounds of typhus seeds, and heaven help anyone they settle on.'

'What's it like? Is it like the plague?' asked Emil. Krösa-Maja had told him about the plague. She kept track of all kinds of diseases and epidemics, and she had told him that the plague was a ghastly thing which once upon a time, a long time ago, had killed nearly everybody in Småland. Just think if typhus was as bad as that!

Krösa-Maja thought for a moment.

'Oh yes, it's rather like the plague,' she said with satisfaction. 'I'm not quite sure, but I seem to remember that first you get blue in the face and then you die. Oh yes, typhus is a terrible disease. Oh, dear me yes.'

But then Emil told her about Lina's toothache and how her cheeks were all swollen just when they were going to have an after-church coffee party, so Krösa-Maja promised to come to Katthult as fast as her legs would carry her.

Emil went home and found Lina sitting on the kitchen step moaning about her toothache, with Alfred and little Ida standing by helplessly.

'There's only one thing to do, you'll have to go to Sme-Pelle,' said Alfred.

Sme-Pelle was the smith in Lönneberga, and he was the man who pulled aching teeth with his big fearsome pincers.

'How much does he charge for pulling out a tooth?' asked Lina between sniffles.

'A krona an hour,' said Alfred, and Lina shuddered when she realized how expensive it was *and* how long it might take.

Emil thought hard, and then he said, 'I can get rid of your tooth cheaper and quicker. I know exactly what to do.'

Then he explained to Lina and Alfred and little Ida what he was going to do.

'I only need two things—Lukas and a long piece of cobbler's twine. I'll tie the twine round your tooth, Lina, and I'll tie the other end to the back of my belt. Then I'll gallop off on Lukas and *ploff*—out comes the tooth.'

'*Ploff* indeed. Thanks very much,' said Lina. 'There's going to be no galloping off with me!'

But just then her tooth gave a terrible twinge, and that made her change her mind. She gave a deep sigh.

'All right, we'll try it. Lord protect me, oh, poor me!' she said and went to get some twine.

Then Emil did just what he had said. He led Lukas to the kitchen step, and when he had finished tying both ends of the twine, he mounted Lukas. Poor Lina whimpered and moaned when she stood tied up behind the horse's tail. Little Ida trembled, but Alfred said cheerfully, 'Now all we have to do is wait for the *ploff*!'

Emil set off at a gallop.

'It'll soon come now,' said little Ida.

But it didn't. Because Lina set off at a gallop, too. She was so afraid of the *ploff* that would come as soon as the thread was taut that she bolted forward just as fast as Lukas, in a dreadful panic. Emil yelled at her to stop, but it made no difference. Lina ran, the twine hung slack, and there was no *ploff*.

But Emil had made up his mind to help Lina get rid of her tooth, so he headed for the nearest fence and Lukas sailed over it. Lina followed behind and, terrified out of her wits, she sailed over it too. Little Ida was watching and you can be sure that as long as she lived she never forgot the sight of Lina, with her swollen cheeks and bulging eyes and the twine hanging out of her mouth, leaping over the fence and screaming, 'Stop! Stop! I don't want a *ploff*!'

Afterwards Lina was ashamed of herself because she had spoilt everything, but by then it was too late; so she again sat down on the kitchen step, nursing her tooth and looking miserable. But Emil didn't give up.

'I'll have to think of another way,' he said.

'Yes, but can we have one that's not quite so fast,' begged Lina. 'The nasty tooth doesn't *have* to come out with a *ploff*. You can just as well pull it out slowly.'

And after Emil had thought for a moment, he knew how to go about it.

Lina had to sit down on the ground with her back against the big pear tree and, while Alfred and Ida looked on curiously, Emil tied her tightly to the trunk with a strong rope.

'Now see if you can run,' he said. Then he picked up the twine which was still hanging out of Lina's mouth and went with it to the grindstone that Alfred used to sharpen his scythe and Emil's father used to sharpen his axes and knives. He tied the twine to the handle, and then all he had to do was to turn the handle.

'It won't be such a quick *ploff*; it'll only be a *drrrrr*. It'll come out slowly, the way you wanted it to,' said Emil.

Little Ida shuddered, Lina howled, and Emil began to turn the handle. The twine, which at first lay slack on the ground, grew tauter and tauter, and the tauter it got the more terrified Lina became, but she couldn't run this time.

'The *drrrrr* will begin soon,' said little Ida.

But then Lina screamed, 'Stop. I can't stand it!'

And in a flash she whipped out a little pair of scissors from her apron pocket and cut the twine.

Afterwards she was ashamed and more miserable than ever, because she *really did* want to get rid of the tooth. It was all too ridiculous. Emil and Alfred and little Ida were not at all pleased, and Emil said, 'Sit there with your old tooth. I'm not going to bother any more!'

Then Lina said that if Emil would try just once more, she wouldn't do anything silly, cross her heart and swear to die.

'This time the tooth is coming out, even if it's the death of me,' said Lina. 'Bring some more twine.'

Emil agreed to try again, and Alfred and little Ida brightened up when they heard this.

'I still think it's best to do it quickly,' said Emil.

'But it must be done in such a way that you can't spoil it even if you *are* afraid.'

And, inventive as he was, Emil soon hit on a new idea.

'We'll put you up on the roof of the cow shed and then you'll jump on to the haystack, and before you're even halfway down, out comes the tooth—*ploff*!"

'*Ploff*,' said little Ida with a shudder.

But in spite of all her promises, Lina wouldn't climb up on the roof.

'No one but Emil could think of anything quite so horrid,' she said, and remained stubbornly sitting on the kitchen step.

But her tooth was aching more and more, and at last she stood up with a deep sigh. 'All right, we'll try it, even if it kills me.'

Alfred quickly placed a ladder against the gable of the cow shed and Emil climbed up it. Holding the twine firmly in his hand, he led Lina like a dog on a leash. She climbed obediently behind him, although she complained all the time.

Emil also carried a hammer and a strong six-inch nail. As soon as he had hammered the nail firmly into the ridge, he tied the loose end of the twine to it, and everything was ready.

'Now jump,' ordered Emil.

Poor Lina, she sat astride the ridge and when she looked down she let out a heart-rending cry. She could see Alfred and little Ida down there with their faces looking up at her. They were waiting for her to come flying down from heaven like a comet and land in the haystack.

Then Lina's wailing became even more desperate, 'I can't. I can't!'

'All right, if you want to keep your old tooth, I don't care,' said Emil.

That caused Lina to bellow so loudly that she could be heard all over Lönneberga. Then she stood up on trembling legs at the very edge of the rooftop, swaying backwards and forwards like a fir tree in a storm. Little Ida covered her eyes with her hands; she dared not look.

'Oh dear, oh dear!' wailed Lina.

Jumping from the cow-shed roof would be terrible even without a sore tooth, but as she knew that there was going to be a horrible *ploff* halfway down, it was almost more than Lina could bear.

'Jump, Lina,' shouted Alfred, 'jump!'

Lina moaned and shut her eyes.

'I'll start you off,' said Emil, like the nice boy he was. All he had to do was give her a little poke in the back with one finger, and she sailed off the roof with a shrill scream.

Sure enough there was a little *ploff*, but it was only the six-inch nail coming out of the rooftop.

Lina lay in the haystack with her tooth still safe and sound in her mouth and the nail hanging on the other end of the twine.

Now she was cross with Emil. 'You can think up your tricks all right, but when it comes to pulling teeth, you're no good at all.'

However, it was a good thing that Lina got cross, for she went straight off to Sme-Pelle in a fury. He gripped the tooth in his fearsome pincers, and it came out with a *ploff*. Afterwards Lina threw it away in Sme-Pelle's junkyard and marched off home.

You mustn't think that Emil was idle in the meantime. Alfred had lain down to sleep in the grass under the pear tree, so he was no fun at the moment. Emil went into the bedroom to play with little Ida, while they were waiting for Father and Mother to come home and begin the after-church party.

'Let's pretend I'm the doctor from Mariannelund,' said Emil, 'and you're the little sick child I have to cure.'

Ida agreed at once. She took off her clothes and got into bed, and Emil looked at her throat and listened to her chest and behaved just like the doctor from Mariannelund.

'What's wrong with me?' asked Ida.

Emil thought for a moment and suddenly had an idea.

'You've got typhus,' he said. 'It's a terrible disease.'

Then he remembered what Krösa-Maja had

said—that you got blue in the face when you had typhus. And, being thorough about such things, Emil looked round for something to make Ida the right colour. On the desk he saw his mother's inkwell, the one she used when she recorded Emil's tricks in her exercise books and when she wrote letters inviting people to after-church coffee. An extra copy of the letter of invitation was also on the desk. Emil read the bit about 'you are cordially invited' and was full of admiration because his mother could write so well and express herself so elegantly. Very different from Adrian who could only manage to write that he had 'seed a bear'.

His mother would not need the extra copy any more, so Emil crumpled the paper into a little ball which he dropped into the inkwell. Then, when it was soaked with ink, he pulled it out and went to Ida, holding it carefully between his fingers and thumb.

'Now you'll see what typhus is like,' he said, and little Ida giggled with delight.

'Shut your eyes tight so that the ink doesn't get into them,' said Emil, and then he painted Ida's face a beautiful blue. But, thoughtful boy that he was, he left two big white circles around her eyes, which made her look so terribly ill that Emil was just a little bit frightened.

'Ugh!' said Emil. 'Krösa-Maja was right. Typhus is a terrible disease.'

Meanwhile, Krösa-Maja had been hobbling along through the forest, and when she came to the path leading to Katthult she met Lina on her way back from Sme-Pelle.

'How's your tooth?' asked Krösa-Maja, eagerly.

'I don't know,' answered Lina.

'What do you mean, you don't know?'

'Well, it's lying in Sme-Pelle's junkyard, the skunk! But I hope it's hurting so much that it's screaming its insides out.'

Lina was feeling more cheerful, and her face was not as swollen as before. She went to the pear tree to show Alfred the hole in her mouth.

Krösa-Maja went into the kitchen to start getting the coffee ready. She could hear the children in the bedroom and wanted to say hello to little Ida who was her favourite, but when she saw her darling propped up against the white pillow and blue in the face, she exclaimed, 'What on earth?'

'It's typhus,' smirked Emil.

At that moment the noise of carts coming down the road could be heard. They were coming from church, Emil's father and mother and all their guests, with the parson himself at the head of the group. When they had tethered the horses down by the stables, they walked up to the farmhouse in a gay procession, eagerly looking forward to the coffee party.

But Krösa-Maja appeared on the step and uttered a piercing shriek, 'Go away all of you! There's typhus in the house.'

Everyone stood still in dismay, but Emil's mother said, 'What are you talking about? Who's got typhus?'

Suddenly little Ida appeared behind Krosa-Maja in the doorway. She was wearing her nightdress, and her face was blue all over, except for the two white circles.

'I have,' she said and giggled merrily.

Everyone began to laugh—everyone except Emil's father. He only said loudly, 'Where's Emil?'

But Emil had disappeared. There was no sign of him during the entire coffee party.

After coffee, the parson went out into the kitchen to comfort Krösa-Maja who sat there sulking because it wasn't really typhus. Then came the extraordinary part. When the parson had finished comforting her, he happened to catch sight of Emil's bundle of letters which was lying on a chair.

He said, 'Ha!' and snatched up the letter which had come from Adrian in America.

'I can't believe it. You've got the very stamp I've been looking for for so long.'

You see, the parson was a stamp collector, and he knew what rare stamps were worth. He offered forty kronor on the spot for the stamp on Adrian's letter.

Emil's father gasped when he heard the dreadful sum. Imagine paying forty kronor for a little scrap of paper like that! He shook his head, almost provoked—it was Emil's usual luck, of course. Now the old velvet-covered box was turning out to be a good buy, too—the best buy that Emil had made at the auction the day before.

'I can buy half a cow for forty kronor,' said Emil's father, resentfully.

Then Emil could not bear to stay hidden in the woodbin any longer. He lifted up the lid and stuck his head out and asked inquisitively, 'If you're going to buy half a cow, are you going to buy the front end that moos or the back end that swishes its tail?'

'Emil, go to the tool shed,' thundered his father.

Emil went, but not before the parson had given him four lovely new ten-kronor notes. And next day he went to see the people at Backhorva and gave them half the money and returned Adrian's letters, and then he rode home with their blessings to continue his little tricks.

'I think I'll travel round to quite a few auctions,' he said when he got home. 'Don't you think it would be a good idea, Father?'

His father mumbled something, though no one could hear what he said.

But the whole of Sunday afternoon after the coffee party Emil stayed in the tool shed carving his one hundred and thirtieth wooden man; until he suddenly remembered that it was Sunday and that you shouldn't use a knife, for it was a terrible sin. Probably you shouldn't try to pull teeth or paint people blue, either. Emil put his wooden man on the shelf with the others. He sat on the chopping block while the darkness fell outside and thought about his sins. Finally he put his hands together and prayed, 'Dear God, Emil Svensson of Katthult, Lönneberga, cordially invites you to stop him playing his tricks.'

*Tuesday, the tenth of August, when Emil put the
frog in the lunch basket and then behaved so badly
that I hardly dare write about it.*

One can't help feeling a bit sorry for Emil's father. One after the other of his son's idiotic bargains had turned out successfully, while all *he* had brought home from the auction was a sow. And just fancy, the horrible creature had eleven piglets one night when no one was expecting it and gobbled up ten of them, for that's what sows do sometimes. The eleventh piglet would have died, too, if Emil hadn't saved it. Emil woke up that night with a stomach ache and had to go out. As he passed the pigsty he heard a baby pig inside squealing for dear life. Emil forced the door open. He had arrived in the nick of time and snatched the last little pig from its cruel mother. She really was a vicious old sow, but anyway, she caught some strange disease and died three days later. Poor Emil's father, now all he had left from the auction at Backhorva was one little piglet.

'There's nothing but misery and misfortune at Backhorva,' he said to Emil's mother when they were in bed that night. 'There's some sort of curse on their animals, that's obvious.'

Emil heard this from his bed and poked his nose out over the sheets.

'I'll take the piglet,' he said. 'I don't mind if there's a curse on it.'

But Emil's father didn't like that kind of talk.

'You're always wanting more and more,' he said bitterly. 'What about me? Am I never going to get anything?'

Emil kept quiet after that and didn't mention the piglet for some time. It was an unusually weak little thing, shivering and sickly.

'It must be the curse that has taken the strength out of it,' said Emil to himself. He thought it was awful how something like that could happen to a little pig that had done no harm to anyone.

Emil's mother thought so, too.

'Poor little beast,' she said.

Lina was fond of animals, too, and especially of this piglet.

'Poor little piggy-beast,' she said. 'He's sure to die soon.'

And he certainly would have, if Emil hadn't taken him into the kitchen and been just like a mother to him. He fed the little pig milk from a baby's bottle, wrapped him in a soft blanket, and put him to bed in a basket.

Alfred came up and watched Emil trying to feed the poor little thing and asked, 'How's he doing?'

'There's a curse on him and he won't eat,' said Emil. 'But we'll see about that. Curse or no curse, I'm going to keep this piglet alive. I've made up my mind.'

And that's exactly what he did! It wasn't long before the pig was a lively little creature and as round and rosy as a little pig should be.

'Little piggy-beast, I really think you're going to be all right,' said Lina. 'Little Piggy-Beast,' she said, and the name stuck to him for the rest of his life.

'Yes, he's going to be all right,' said Emil's father. 'You've done a good job, Emil.'

Emil was pleased when his father praised him, and he promptly asked, 'How many times must I save his life before I get him?'

Emil's father only said, 'Hmm' and looked stern, so Emil kept quiet and didn't mention the pig for some time.

Now Piggy-Beast was put out in the pigsty again, but he didn't like it very much. What he liked was to trot round at Emil's heels just like a dog, and Emil nearly always allowed him to tag along.

'He thinks you're his mummy,' said little Ida, and perhaps Piggy-Beast did think so, for as soon as he saw Emil he would rush towards him squealing with joy. He wanted to be with Emil; he wanted to have his back scratched now and then, and Emil always did it for him.

'I've got the knack of scratching pigs,' he said, as he sat comfortably on the bench under the cherry tree and gave Piggy-Beast a good old scratch. Piggy-Beast stood there with his eyes shut and grunted now and then to show how much he was enjoying himself.

The summer days came and went. The cherries ripened on the tree above the spot where Piggy-Beast stood to be scratched. Sometimes Emil pulled off a handful of cherries and gave them to Piggy-Beast who liked cherries as much as he liked Emil. The pig became quite convinced that a pig could have a fine life if he happened to be in a

place where there was an Emil.

Emil liked Piggy-Beast, too, more and more every day. Once when he was sitting on the bench scratching Piggy-Beast's back, he began to think how *much* he really liked him, and that made him think about the other people he liked.

Alfred comes first, he thought, then Lukas, then Ida, and then Piggy-Beast—but, oh, I've forgotten Mummy—it's obvious about Mummy—of course, but otherwise it's Alfred and Lukas and Ida and Piggy-Beast.

Then he puckered his eyebrows and thought hard.

That leaves Papa and Lina, he thought. There are some days when I like Papa and there are some days when I don't. I just don't know about Lina, I don't like her and I don't dislike her. I pay as little attention to her as I do to the cat.

Naturally, Emil went on getting into mischief every day, and he spent a lot of time in the tool shed, as we can see from the blue exercise books. But Emil's mother was very busy because of the harvest and sometimes she only wrote: 'Emil in the tool shed,' without saying why.

Now Emil had started taking Piggy-Beast to the tool shed with him, because the time goes much quicker with a playful little pig for company, and after all he couldn't carve little wooden men all the time. Instead, he began to train Piggy-Beast to do all kinds of tricks that no one would have believed an ordinary little Småland pig could possibly do. It was all very secret and Piggy-Beast enjoyed himself and learnt very quickly, especially because each time he did something well he got a titbit from Emil. Emil had a whole stock of biscuits and cakes and dried cherries in a secret box behind the carpenter's bench; since he never knew when he might have to go to the tool shed, he didn't want to sit there and die of starvation.

'If you're clever at it and you've got some dried cherries, you can teach a little pig anything,' Emil explained to Alfred and Ida, one Saturday evening when he decided to reveal Piggy-Beast's secret skills, which no one had been allowed to see before. Every one was in the lilac grove, and it was a great moment for both Emil and Piggy-Beast. Alfred and Ida sat on a bench and opened their eyes wide with astonishment when they saw the marvellous things Piggy-Beast could do. They had never seen such a pig. He could sit just like a dog, when Emil said 'Sit,' and pretend to be dead, when Emil said 'Dead pig,' and hold out his right foot in thanks, when Emil gave him dried cherries.

Ida clapped her hands with delight.

'Can he do anything else?' she asked excitedly.

Then Emil shouted 'Gallop,' and, whoops, Piggy-Beast started to run round the lilac grove. Every now and then Emil shouted 'Jump' and Piggy-Beast

leapt straight up in the air and then went on running again, looking extremely pleased with himself.

'Oh, how sweet,' said little Ida, and he did look very sweet going round and round, making his little jumps in the lilac grove.

'All the same, it's not natural for a pig,' said Alfred, but Emil was proud and pleased because he was sure there wasn't another pig like Piggy-Beast in the whole of Lönneberga and the whole of Småland.

Gradually, Emil taught Piggy-Beast to skip as well. Have you ever seen a pig skip? No, you haven't? Well, Emil's father hadn't either. But one day when he was walking down by the cow pasture he saw Emil and Ida swinging an old bridle rein as Piggy-Beast jumped over it, with his little feet spreading out at every jump.

'He thinks it's fun,' little Ida assured him, but her father wasn't impressed.

'Pigs aren't meant to have fun,' he said. 'They're meant for Christmas hams and with all that skipping it's going to be as thin as a whippet. Now let that be the last of it.'

Emil gave a cold shudder. Christmas ham out of Piggy-Beast, he hadn't thought about that, but now he did and he decided it was one of the days when he didn't really like his father very much.

The day when Emil didn't like his father very much was Tuesday, August 10. It was early in the morning of what was going to be a hot summer day when Piggy-Beast skipped in the cow pasture and Emil's father made the remark about the Christmas ham. Then he went away, for that was the very day when they were going to begin the rye harvest at Katthult, and Emil's father was going to be out in the fields until nightfall.

'Whatever you do, Piggy-Beast,' said Emil, when his father had gone, 'keep as thin as a whippet, then you might be all right. You don't know my father like I do.'

Emil worried about Piggy-Beast all day and only had the heart to play a few little tricks which weren't very serious. He sat Ida in the old wooden trough where they watered the horses and cows and pretended it was a boat in the sea. Then he pumped the trough full of water and pretended it was a boat which was leaking badly, and Ida got soaking wet, which she thought was great fun. Next Emil fired his catapult at a bowl of rhubarb cream which his mother had left to cool on the windowsill. He only wanted to see if he could hit it, he hadn't expected it to break; but it did, and he was glad his father was far away in the rye field.

His mother only made him sit in the tool shed for a short time, partly because she felt sorry for him and partly because she wanted him to take the basket of coffee and sandwiches to the harvesters. The harvesters had their coffee in the field because it was the custom in the whole of Lönneberga and the whole of Småland, and it was also the custom for the children from the farms to take the basket with the hot coffee and sandwiches in it out to them.

The Småland children looked like angelic messengers carrying their baskets along the winding paths that ended up at little fields so full of stones that you could cry. But the Småland children didn't cry, because wild strawberries grew among the stones, and they loved wild strawberries.

That day Emil and Ida set off from home in good time, carrying the basket between them. But Emil could never go directly to a place. He always had to turn off here, there and everywhere, wherever there was anything interesting to look at. And wherever Emil went, Ida went too. One of his detours was down to a swamp where frogs could usually be found and, just as he had expected, there was one there that day. He wanted to study it more closely; besides, he thought it could probably do with a change of scenery after sitting in the swamp all day. So he put it into the basket, and shut the lid to keep it safe.

'Where else can I keep it?' said Emil when Ida wondered whether the basket was the right place for it. 'There's a hole in my trouser pocket, you know. Besides, it won't be there for long. I'll soon put it back in the swamp again,' said the reasonable boy.

Far away in the field, Emil's father and Alfred were working away with their scythes and behind them came Lina and Krösa-Maja, gathering up the cut rye and tying it into sheaves. That was the way it was done in those days.

When Emil and Ida finally appeared with the lunch, Emil's father didn't greet them as ministering angels, but lectured them for arriving so late. You see, it was very important that they got their coffee on time.

'A cup of coffee would go down well now,' said Alfred, trying to distract Emil's father.

If you have ever been in the fields of Lönneberga during a coffee break on a warm August day, you know how nice it can be to sit on a sunny pile of stones, resting and chatting and drinking coffee and eating sandwiches. But Emil's father was still feeling cross, and it didn't improve matters when he picked up the basket and lifted the lid, because the frog jumped straight at him and disappeared inside his shirt, which was unbuttoned because of the heat. The little frog's feet were so cold that Emil's father shuddered all over. He swung his arms about and, alas, he knocked over the coffeepot; but Emil was there in a flash and picked it up so that only a little of the coffee was spilt. There was no sign of the frog because in its fright it had tried to hide deeper in Emil's father's trousers. When Emil's father felt it, he went absolutely frantic and kicked out in all directions. Unfortunately, the coffeepot was in the way again and it got kicked over. If Emil hadn't been there again in a flash, there would have been a coffee break without any coffee, which would have been very sad.

The frog obviously didn't like being where it was and, as it slid out of Emil's father's trouser leg, Emil

grabbed it. But Emil's father was still as angry as ever. He thought that the frog was one of Emil's usual tricks, but of course it wasn't. Emil had expected Lina, not his father, to open the basket and be quite enchanted when she saw such a dear little frog. So you see how sometimes it was rather hard for Emil, because he was blamed for playing tricks when he hadn't meant anything at all. Where did Emil's father think he was supposed to keep the frog, anyway, as there were holes in both of his trouser pockets?

Lina was saying, 'I've never seen the like of that boy for playing tricks, and if he doesn't play them, they seem to happen on their own just because he's there.'

Lina had never said truer words. The catastrophe

later that same day proved it. Emil got into such trouble that I can hardly bear to tell you about it, and the whole of Lönneberga shook their heads for a long time afterwards. Really, it was all because his mother was such a good housewife and there were so many cherries at Katthult that year, but what could he do about that?

No one was better than Emil's mother at making jelly and jams and syrups and preserves from the things which grew wild or in the garden. She picked all the red whortleberries and blueberries and raspberries she could; then she made apple cheese and pear ginger and currant jelly and gooseberry jelly and cherry syrup. She dried enough fruit to last through the winter and use in her good fruit soups. The apples and pears and cherries were dried in the big kitchen oven and then tied up in white linen cloths which Emil's mother hung from the ceiling of the storeroom. Yes, the storeroom was a joy to see.

At the busiest time of the cherry season, grand

Mrs Petrell from Vimmerby had paid a visit to Katthult and while she was there Emil's mother complained that there were so many blessed cherries she didn't know what to do with them.

'What you should do is make cherry wine,' said Mrs Petrell.

'Goodness me, no!' exclaimed Emil's mother. Cherry wine was quite out of the question, since Katthult was against strong drink. Emil's father never drank anything strong; he didn't even drink beer except when he couldn't help it because it was forced upon him at the markets and places like that. After all, what was he to do when someone invited him to have a drink or even two drinks maybe. He was quick to note that two bottles of beer cost thirty öre and you can't throw away thirty öre just like that.

All he could do was drink the beer, whether he liked it or not. But Emil's mother knew that he would never let her make cherry wine, and she told Mrs Petrell. But Mrs Petrell said that even if no one at Katthult drank wine, there might be others who didn't mind an occasional glass. She for one would be very pleased to have a couple of bottles of cherry wine; so why couldn't Emil's mother just put a large jar of cherries to ferment in some far corner of the potato cellar where no one would see it. When it had finished fermenting, she would come back and fetch the wine and pay a good price for it, she said.

It was always difficult for Emil's mother to say no when anyone asked her to do anything, and, as we have said, she was a very good housewife who didn't like to waste anything. There were more dried cherries than she knew what to do with, and somehow without knowing quite how, she promised to make the cherry wine for Mrs Petrell. But Emil's mother wasn't the sort of person to do anything on the sly. She told Emil's father all about it and he argued a lot, but in the end he said, 'Do just as you like. How much did you say she would pay?'

Mrs Petrell hadn't actually said how much.

Now it was August 10. The wine had been fermenting in the potato cellar for several weeks, and

Emil's mother decided it was ready. Now it was time to bottle it. She thought it was best to do this while Emil's father was out in the rye field, then he wouldn't see her doing it and feel sinful and wicked because he had allowed wine to be made in his house.

Emil's mother soon had ten bottles of wine lined up on the kitchen table. She was going to pack them in a basket and hide it in a corner of the potato cellar where no one need feel guilty about it, and then Mrs Petrell could come and fetch her wine when she wanted.

The cherries used to make the wine were in a bucket outside the kitchen door when Emil and Ida came home from the rye field with the basket.

'Take the bucket, Emil,' said Emil's mother, 'and go and bury these cherries in the rubbish heap, please.'

Obedient boy that he was, Emil went off, but the rubbish heap was just behind the pigsty where Piggy-Beast was wandering about. When he saw Emil, he grunted loudly to let him know that he wanted to be let out of his pen and follow Emil round.

'All right,' said Emil, and put down the bucket. He opened the little door to the pigsty, and Piggy-Beast ran out with a joyful grunt. He stuck his snout straight into the bucket, for he thought that Emil had brought him food. It was only then that Emil began to wonder why his mother had told him to bury the cherries in the rubbish heap. It was very strange because at Katthult no one ever buried anything that was good to eat, and the cherries were obviously good. Piggy-Beast had already gobbled up quite a lot. Emil decided that the reason his mother wanted the cherries buried in the rubbish heap was to get them out of the way before his father came back from the rye field.

Piggy-Beast might just as well eat them then, thought Emil. He loves cherries.

Piggy-Beast seemed to like these cherries better than any, for he grunted with delight and ate until he was red in the snout. To make it easier for him, Emil poured the cherries on the ground. Then the cock came along and wanted to join the feast.

Piggy-Beast glared at him, but allowed him to stay and peck away at the berries as fast as he could. Then the hens came, with Lame Lotta leading, to see what titbits the cock had found. But they weren't allowed near, for as soon as they stuck out their beaks, Piggy-Beast and the cock drove them away mercilessly. It was clear that the cock and Piggy-Beast intended to keep these especially good cherries for themselves.

Emil was sitting close by on the upturned bucket, trying to blow a sound on a blade of grass that he  held between his thumbs and thinking about nothing in particular. Then to his surprise he suddenly saw the cock fall over. It made several attempts to stand on its feet again, but without success. As soon as it got halfway up, it fell forward again and lay flat on its face. The hens stood in a cluster a short distance away, watching the curious behaviour of their lord and master and clucking anxiously. This irritated the cock lying on the ground and he glared ferociously. Couldn't a fellow lie about where he wanted?

Emil couldn't understand what had got into the cock, but he felt sorry for him and picked him up and put him on his feet. The cock stood there for a moment, swaying backwards and forwards, but then some sort of madness got into him. First he crowed, then he flapped his wings arrogantly, and then he rushed towards the hens. They fled as fast as they could, for they could see that the cock had gone crazy. Emil could see this too, and he was so amazed by the cock's wild rampaging that he didn't notice Piggy-Beast. Talk about madness, if anyone had gone stark-raving mad, it was Piggy-Beast!

He thought it was a lovely idea to go chasing the hens, so he charged forward on the heels of the cock, grunting loudly. Emil was completely baffled,

he couldn't understand
what was going on. Piggy-
Beast's grunts were loud
and fierce. He seemed to
be enjoying himself, but
Emil could see that there
was something wrong
with his legs. They wob-
bled all over the place,
and he seemed to have no

control over them. He would certainly have fallen
over like the cock if he hadn't given one of those
little jumps, like Emil taught him, every time he was
at the point of collapsing. The little jumps seemed
to help him keep his balance.

The poor hens, they had never seen a pig behaving
like this before, and they fled for their lives. Their
terrified cackles were pitiful to hear, poor things. It
was bad enough that their cock had gone mad, but
a ferocious pig with glaring red eyes bounding after
them, that was too much.

Yes, it was too much. Emil knew about being so terrified that you died of fright, and he suddenly saw one hen after the other collapse and lie motionless. All the grass was covered with dead hens lying there white and still. It was a terrible sight. Emil was in despair and began to cry. What would his mother say when she found her hens like this? Lame Lotta, his own hen, lay there, too, in a dead white lump, and Emil sobbed as he picked her up. There was no sign of life in her, she was quite dead. Poor Lame Lotta, that was the end of her and all her lovely eggs. There was nothing Emil could do except give her a decent burial as quickly as possible. He could already see the inscription on her tombstone: 'Here rests Lame Lotta, frightened to death by Piggy-Beast.'

Emil was really furious with Piggy-Beast. He was going to lock the monster in the pigsty and never let him out again. But before that he decided to put Lame Lotta in the woodshed. He carried her there very carefully and laid her on the chopping block where she could wait for her burial, poor Lotta!

When he came out of the woodshed, he saw that the cock and Piggy-Beast were eating the cherries again. They were fine ones! They frightened the hens to death and then went calmly back to the feast as if nothing had happened. At least the cock could have had the decency to mourn a little when he'd lost all his wives in one fell swoop, but he didn't seem the slightest bit upset.

The cherry feast never really got going again, because the cock fell over immediately and Piggy-Beast soon after him. Emil was so mad at them and he didn't care if they were alive or dead, and anyway he could see that they weren't as dead as the hens. The cock clucked weakly and moved its legs about, and Piggy-Beast lay there half asleep, grunting hoarsely and trying to open his eyes now and then.

There were still lots of cherries lying on the ground and Emil tried one. They didn't taste the way cherries usually do, but the truth was that they weren't at all bad. Whatever made his mother think of burying such delicious cherries?

Oh yes—Mamma—he'd have to go and tell her about the disaster. He didn't really feel like doing it just at the moment. He ate a few more cherries while he thought about it—and then a few more—no, he didn't want to tell her just yet!

By this time Emil's mother had prepared supper in the kitchen for the harvesters. Soon Emil's father, Alfred, Lina, and Krösa-Maja came home, all very tired and hungry after a long day's work. They sat round the kitchen table; but Emil's place was empty, and Emil's mother remembered that she hadn't seen her son for some time.

'Lina, go and see if Emil's out with Piggy-Beast,' said Emil's mother.

Lina left and was away for quite a while. When

she finally came back, she stood in the doorway waiting until they were all looking at her. She wanted to have everyone's attention while she told her dreadful tale.

'What's the matter? Why are you standing there like that? Is something wrong?' asked Emil's mother.

Lina smiled to herself.

'Is anything wrong! I don't know where to begin. The hens are dead that's one thing, and the cock's

drunk, and Piggy-Beast is drunk, and as for Emil, well—'

'What's the matter with Emil?' asked Emil's mother, anxiously.

'Emil,' said Lina taking a deep breath, 'Emil is drunk too.'

I can hardly tell you what it was like that night at Katthult.

Emil's father ranted and shouted. Emil's mother and little Ida wept, and Lina wept to keep them company.

Krösa-Maja rocked and wailed and didn't stop to finish her supper, for she was in such a hurry to go round the village and tell everyone.

'Deary, deary me!' she said. 'The poor Svenssons at Katthult. That terrible boy, Emil, has got drunk and killed all the hens. Oh dear, oh dear.'

Alfred was the only one to remain fairly calm. He rushed out with the others when Lina came with the shocking news and found Emil lying on the grass beside Piggy-Beast and the cock. Yes, Lina was right, Emil was certainly drunk. He lay there, slumped heavily against Piggy-Beast, his eyes were out of focus, and it was obvious that he wasn't well. Emil's mother burst into loud tears when she saw her poor unfortunate boy and wanted to carry him straight to bed.

But Alfred, who knew about these things, said, 'He's better out in the fresh air.'

Alfred sat on the steps outside his hut all evening with Emil in his arms. He helped him when he felt sick and comforted him when he cried, for Emil woke up sometimes and cried with shame. He had heard them say that he was drunk, though he couldn't understand how it had happened. Emil did not know that when you make wine out of cherries and let them ferment for a long time they get soaked full of something that makes people drunk. That was why Emil's mother had told him to bury the cherries in the rubbish heap; but instead he and the cock and Piggy-Beast had eaten them, and that was why he was now lying wretchedly in Alfred's arms.

He lay there for a long time. The sun set, night came, and the moon rose over Katthult, and Alfred still sat there with Emil.

'How are you feeling, Emil?' asked Alfred, when he saw Emil moving his eyelids a little.

'I'm not dead yet,' Emil said in a faint voice. And then he whispered, 'If I do die, you can have Lukas.'

'You're not going to die,' Alfred assured him.

No, Emil didn't die; neither did Piggy-Beast nor the cock.

And neither did the hens. That was the strange thing. What happened was that in the middle of all the trouble, Emil's mother sent little Ida to fetch a basket of wood. Ida was crying as she went, for everything about tonight was sad, and she cried even more when she entered the woodshed and saw Lame Lotta lying there on the chopping block.

'Poor Lotta,' said Ida, as her tiny hand stroked Lotta, and believe it or not—Lotta came to life. She opened her eyes and with an irritable clucking,

fluttered down from the chopping block and limped crossly out through the door. Ida stood still in surprise and didn't know what to think. Perhaps she had magic hands which could bring the dead back to life.

Everyone had been so upset about Emil that no one had bothered about the hens that were still out on the grass. So then little Ida came along and stroked each one of them in turn and every single hen came to life again and leapt up. They weren't dead, but had only fainted from fright after being chased by Piggy-Beast, for hens do that sometimes.

But Ida went proudly into the kitchen where her mother and father sat moaning. Now she, too, had some important news.

'Well, anyway, I've brought the hens back to

life again,' she said, looking very pleased with herself.

The cock, Piggy-Beast, and Emil all felt a little better next morning. But the cock couldn't crow for three days. He tried now and then, but instead of a beautiful cock-a-doodle-doo, all that came out was a nasty cracked noise which made him very embarrassed. Each time the hens would look at him disapprovingly, and then he would go and hide in the bushes, feeling very ashamed of himself.

Piggy-Beast wasn't at all ashamed, but Emil looked guilty all day, and Lina continually rubbed it in.

'Lying down drunk with a pig, indeed! Drunken swine, that's what you and Piggy-Beast are, and that's what I shall call you after this.'

'That's enough of that now,' said Alfred, looking at her sternly, and then she stopped.

But that wasn't the end of the story. Early that afternoon, in through the gate at Katthult came three solemn men, three Good Templars from the Lönneberga Order of Good Templars. I don't suppose you've ever heard of the Order of Good Templars, but I can tell you that it was very necessary in Lönneberga and the whole of Småland in those days. The Good Templars did their best to stop the dreadful drunkenness that caused so many people unhappiness and still does, come to think of it.

It was Krösa-Maja's gossiping about Emil's drunkenness that had set the Order of Good Templars in motion. Now they had come to the farm, asking to talk to Emil's father and mother. They said it would be a good idea if Emil could come to the meeting at the Good Templars' Hall that evening and be converted to a sober life. Emil's mother was livid with rage and told them exactly what had happened with Emil and the cherries.

But the three Good Templars still looked worried, and one of them said, 'All the same, we can all see how Emil is shaping up. It would not do him any harm to hear the good word tonight.'

Emil's father agreed with them. He was not happy. It wouldn't be pleasant to stand in front of all those people at the meeting, feeling ashamed of his own son; but perhaps it was necessary to go, if Emil were to be put on a more sober track.

'I'll take him along,' muttered Emil's father, gloomily.

'If anyone goes with him, I'll go,' said Emil's mother, for she had plenty of courage. 'I'm the one who made the wretched wine, so why should Anton suffer for it. I'm the one who needs a temperance sermon, but Emil can come along too if you think he really ought to.'

In the evening Emil had to put on his Sunday clothes and his cap. He didn't mind going to be converted. It might be quite fun to go out and see all the people.

Piggy-Beast thought so, too. When Emil and his mother started off Piggy-Beast came running after them and wanted to go. But Emil said 'Dead pig,' and Piggy-Beast lay obediently in the road and was quite still, although his eyes followed Emil for a long time.

The Good Templars' Hall was crowded that night, I can tell you. The whole of Lönneberga wanted to help in the conversion of Emil. The choir was lined up on the platform at the back of the hall, and as soon as Emil came through the door they started to sing very loudly:

O you, young man, who drank the glass with deadly poison in it—

'It *wasn't* a glass,' Emil's mother said crossly, but only Emil heard her.

When the song was over, a man stepped forward and gave Emil a long serious talk, and finally asked him if he would take a pledge to stay sober for the rest of his life.

'I don't mind,' said Emil.

Just at that moment a little grunt was heard and through the door trotted Piggy-Beast. He had followed Emil, without Emil knowing it, and now here he was. He was pleased when he caught sight of

Emil in the front row and ran straight to him. There was a great commotion, for there had never been a pig in the Good Templars' Hall before, and they didn't want one there now. It wasn't at all fitting to have a pig in a place like this.

But Emil said, 'He needs to take a pledge as well. He ate more cherries than I did.'

Piggy-Beast seemed to be a bit over excited, so Emil said 'Sit,' and, to everyone's astonishment, Piggy-Beast sat on his hind legs just like a dog. He looked very sweet and proper. Emil took some dried cherries out of his pocket and gave them to him, and the people of Lönneberga couldn't believe their eyes when the pig stuck his right foot forward in a gesture of thanks.

Everyone was so fascinated by Piggy-Beast that

they almost forgot about the temperance pledge. Emil himself had to remind them.

'Well, am I supposed to be making this promise or not?'

Then Emil promised 'to abstain from strong liquor in the future and also to work in whatever manner he could for the increased sobriety of his fellow men.'

'That goes for you, too, Piggy-Beast,' said Emil, after he had made his promise.

Later everyone in Lönneberga said that no one had ever taken a temperance pledge at the same time as a pig. 'But that Katthult boy is an unusual one,' they said.

When Emil arrived home and went into the kitchen with Piggy-Beast at his heels, his father was sitting by himself near the lit paraffin lamp. Emil could see that he had been crying. Emil had never seen his father cry before, and he didn't like it, but then his father said something which Emil did like.

'Listen, Emil,' he said, taking the lad by the shoulders and looking him straight in the eye. 'Emil, if you promise to be sober all your life, you can have that cursed pig—anyway, there can't be any good meat on it after all that skipping and drunkenness.'

Emil was so overcome that he jumped for joy. Once again he promised to be sober all his life and he kept the promise, too. No one had ever seen such a sober president of the council as Emil became, and so perhaps it wasn't such a bad thing that he ate fermented cherries one summer day when he was little.

That night Emil lay awake a long time talking to Ida.

'Now I've got a horse and a cow and a pig and a hen,' he said.

'But don't forget I brought the hen back to life,' said little Ida, and Emil thanked her for doing that.

He woke up early next morning and heard Alfred and Lina talking while they drank their coffee in the kitchen; so he jumped straight out of bed, because he couldn't wait to tell Alfred that he could keep Piggy-Beast.

'Animal owner, Emil Svensson,' said Alfred, and chuckled. But Lina tossed her head and chanted a little rhyme which she had been making up while she was doing the milking. This is how it went:

His mother took him to the Good Templars' Hall
There they made a man out of a drunken swine.
He's promised that he'll never be drunk any more
And they've given him the pig he was before.

A more stupid song you couldn't imagine. 'They've given him the pig he was before' was very silly, but that was just like Lina, she couldn't do any better.

Then it was time for Alfred and Lina to go back to the rye field again with Emil's father and Krösa-Maja.

Emil's mother stayed at home with the children.

She was quite glad to be on her own, because that was the day when Mrs Petrell was to come and fetch her bottles of wine, and Emil's mother didn't want Emil's father to be round then.

It will be a relief to have the bottles out of the house, thought Emil's mother, as she busied herself in the kitchen. Mrs Petrell might arrive at any minute and she listened for the sound of cart wheels on the road. But what she heard was something quite different—a crash like broken glass from the potato cellar.

She looked through the window and saw Emil sitting with the poker in his hand and a row of bottles in front of him, and he was smashing them one after the other so that the splinters of glass flew and the wine flowed.

Emil's mother flung open the window and shouted, 'What on earth do you think you're doing, Emil!'

Emil stopped just long enough to answer, 'I'm working for temperance,' he said, 'so I thought I'd begin with Mrs Petrell.'

*Some days in Emil's life, when he got into mischief,
but did a lot of good things, too.*

That wretched cherry wine was one of the things which was remembered in Lönneberga for a long time, though Emil's mother would have preferred to forget it as quickly as possible. She didn't write anything in the blue exercise book about what happened on that fateful August 10. It was so awful that she couldn't bring herself to write about it. But on August 11 she made a note, and when you come across it without any warning, it gives you rather a start.

'Heaven help my poor boy, but at least he was

sober today.' That's all it says, no more and no less. You are left wondering whatever did happen, and whether it was true about Emil seldom being sober. Emil's mother really should have explained what it was all about, but as I have said, she couldn't bring herself to do so.

There is also a note on August 15, when she wrote, 'Last night Emil and Alfred went out to catch crayfish, they caught sixty score, but afterwards, oh dear me—'

Sixty score, have you ever heard anything like it? That is an incredible number of crayfish, I can tell you. Just think about it and you'll realize why Emil enjoyed that night. If you have ever gone fishing for crayfish on some little Småland lake on a dark August night, you will understand why. You will know what fun it is and how wet you get and how strange the world is. Oh, it's so dark and the wood is so black round the lake. Everything is very quiet, and all you can hear is the water splashing against your legs as you wade about near the shore. If you have a torch with you, like Emil and Alfred had, you can see the big black crayfish crawling round between the stones on the bottom of the lake. And you only have to put in your hand and grab hold of their backs, one after the other, and pop them into the sack.

When Emil and Alfred walked slowly home at dawn, they had so many crayfish that they could hardly carry them, but Emil whistled and sang as he walked.

What a lovely surprise for Papa, he thought.

The thing was that Emil liked to show his father what a fine boy he was, but so often it didn't work out that way. He wanted his father to see the mass of crayfish the moment he awoke, so he put them in the big copper cauldron, the one in which he and Ida took their baths on Saturday nights. Then he took it into the bedroom and put it next to his father's bed.

What excitement there will be when they all wake up and see my crayfish, thought Emil. Then he crept into bed, feeling tired and happy, and went to sleep.

All was quiet in the bedroom. The only sounds were little whistling snores from his father and the soft clattering sound of the crayfish crawling all over each other, as crayfish do.

Emil's father got up very early every morning, and he did so this morning. As soon as the wall clock had struck five, he pulled off the bedcovers and slung his legs over the edge of the bed, then sat for a while, until he woke himself up properly. He stretched and yawned and scratched his head and wiggled his toes. He had once had his left big toe caught in a rat trap that Emil had set, and since then the toe was a bit stiff and needed to be loosened up in the morning, and as Emil's father was sitting there loosening it up, he suddenly gave a bellow that made little Ida and Emil's mother wake up in terror. They thought that Emil's father was being murdered at least, but it was only a crayfish which had grabbed him by his big toe, the same toe that had been caught in the rat trap. If you have ever had your big toe in a crayfish's claws, then you'll know it's just about as painful as having it in a rat trap. You just can't help bellowing. Crayfish are stubborn creatures—they hang on for dear life, gripping harder and harder. No wonder that Emil's father screamed. So did Emil's mother and little Ida, after they saw all the hundreds of crayfish crawling about on the floor. Oh yes, there was ever so much excitement that morning.

'Emil,' shrieked Emil's father at the top of his voice, partly because he was angry and partly because he wanted Emil to fetch the pincers so he

could pull the crayfish off his toe. Emil was so sound asleep that he couldn't be woken up by any amount of excitement. Emil's father had to hop on one leg to the toolbox in the kitchen cupboard to get the pincers himself, and when little Ida saw him hopping across the floor with the crayfish dangling from his big toe, she was very upset because it was such a pity that Emil was lying asleep and missing it all.

'Wake up, Emil,' she shouted. 'Wake up if you want to see something funny.'

But she was silent when she saw the look on her father's face. He obviously didn't see anything funny about it.

Meanwhile Emil's mother crawled round on the floor picking up crayfish. After two hours, she had collected all of them. When Emil finally woke up later in the morning, all he noticed was the delicious smell of freshly cooked crayfish drifting in from the kitchen, and he wriggled his legs with pleasure.

For three days they ate crayfish at Katthult and delighted in them. And besides that, Emil cleaned a mass of crayfish tails and sold them to the parson's wife for twenty-five öre a pint. He shared the proceeds with Alfred, who was always short of money and thought Emil quite remarkable to have had the idea.

'You're a smart businessman, Emil,' he said, and he was right about that. Emil already had fifty kronor in his money box that he had earned at different times. Once he had thought about carrying through a really big deal by agreeing to sell all his little wooden men to Mrs Petrell because she loved them so. But fortunately nothing came of it. The wooden men stayed on the shelf and they're still there today. Mrs Petrell also wanted to buy Emil's wooden gun and give it to a horrid little boy she knew, but nothing came of that either. In fact, Emil realized that he was getting too old to play with it, but all the same he didn't want to sell it. Instead he nailed it to the wall of the tool

shed and wrote above it in red crayon: A PRESENT
FROM ALFRED.

Alfred laughed when he saw it, but you could tell
he was pleased.

Emil wore his cap all the time, he couldn't do
without it, and he even wore it the first day he went
to school. Yes, it was time for Emil to start school
and the whole of Lönneberga held its breath.

Lina didn't think school was going to do Emil
much good.

'He'll turn the schoolhouse upside down and set
fire to the teacher,' she said. But Emil's mother
looked sternly at her.

'Emil is a dear little boy,' she said. 'I know he set
fire to the parson's wife the other day, but he's
already sat in the tool shed for that, and there's no
need for you to carry on about it now.'

It was August 17 when Emil sat in the tool shed
because of the parson's wife. That was the day she
came to Katthult to get a weaving pattern from
Emil's mother, and was invited to have some coffee

in the lilac grove while she looked at it. She had weak eyes and took a magnifying glass out of her handbag. Emil had never seen one before, and he was very interested in it.

'You can borrow it if you like,' said the parson's wife in her innocence. She didn't know that Emil could play tricks with absolutely anything, and a magnifying glass was ideal. It didn't take him long to find out that it could be used as a burning glass. When the sun shone on the glass, the rays were concentrated into a single point which shone and smouldered, and Emil looked round for something really inflammable. The parson's wife was calmly sitting there talking away to his mother, and she kept her head erect and still. The ostrich feathers in her elegant hat looked just the thing and Emil tried them, not because he thought it would work, but because he thought that you have to experiment if you are to ever find out anything.

The result of his experiment is described in the blue exercise book: 'A smell of smoke came from the parson's wife, from her feathers I mean; but they did not catch fire properly, they only smelled as if they were burning. And there I was, thinking that Emil was going to behave better now that he is a Good Templar. Well, Mr Good Templar sat in the tool shed for the rest of the day. That's what he did.'

On August 25 Emil started school. If the people of Lönneberga had thought he was going to disgrace himself there, they made a big mistake. The school mistress was the first person who had a feeling that a future president of the local council was sitting on the bench nearest the window, for, wonder of wonders, Emil was top in the class. He could already read before he went to school and write a little too, and he learnt his numbers more quickly than anyone else. Naturally, he got up to lots of mischief as well, but his antics weren't so bad that the mistress couldn't put up with them—well, of course, there was the time that he gave her a smacking kiss on the lips, and they talked about that in Lönneberga for a long time afterwards.

This was what happened. Emil was standing at the blackboard adding up a difficult sum.

When he was finished the school mistress said, 'Good, Emil. You can go and sit down now.'

He did so, but on the way he leaned towards the school mistress and gave her a big kiss on the mouth. Nothing like that had ever happened to her before and she blushed and began to stammer, 'Why—why did you do that, Emil?'

'I did it out of my goodness,' said Emil, and it became almost a saying in Lönneberga after that. 'I did it out of my goodness, as the Katthult boy said when he kissed the school mistress,' they used to say in those days, and perhaps still do today, for all I know.

Afterwards, during the break, one of the big boys came up and started to tease him.

'Look who kissed the mistress,' he sneered.

'Yes, I did,' said Emil. 'Do you want me to do it again?'

But he didn't do it again, it was just that once and

never again. The school mistress wasn't displeased with Emil because of that kiss, far from it.

There were many things which Emil did out of his goodness. During the eleven o'clock break, he used to scamper over to the poorhouse and read the *Småland's Daily News* to Stolle-Jocke and the other old people; so you see that was one of the things he did out of his goodness.

Stolle-Jocke and Johan Ett Öre and Lillklossan and Kalle Spader and all the other old folk thought that it was the nicest time of the day when Emil came. Perhaps Stolle-Jocke didn't always understand very well, because when Emil read that there was going to be a dance at the big hotel in Eksjö on the following Saturday, he clasped his hands devoutly and said, 'Amen, amen, God's will be done.'

But the main thing was that Jocke and all the others liked to sit there and listen to Emil's reading. The only person who didn't like it was the superintendent. She shut herself up in her room in the attic whenever Emil came, because she had once been caught in a wolf pit that Emil had dug, and she had never forgotten it.

Perhaps you're beginning to wonder whether Emil would have time to get into any more mischief now that he was going to school, but you needn't worry. You see, when Emil was little they only had school every other day, the lucky children.

'What are you doing with yourself these days?' asked Stolle-Jocke one day when Emil came to read the paper to him.

Emil thought for a moment and answered truthfully, 'One day I play tricks, and the next day I go to school.'

Sunday, the fourteenth of November, when the parson heard the Catechism at Katthult and Emil locked his father in the Trisse hut.

Autumn had arrived and the days grew greyer and darker at Katthult and in the whole of Lönneberga and the whole of Småland.

'Ugh,' said Lina when she had to go out into the farmyard while it was still dark at five o'clock in the morning. Of course she had a lantern to light her way, but it gave out such a lonely, pathetic light in all the surrounding gloom. Grey, grey, the whole autumn was one long grey weekday, with only an occasional party or catechism hearing to brighten up the darkness.

Of course you've never heard of a catechism hearing, but in those days the people were supposed to know the catechism and the stories in the Bible quite well. And so the parson had to hear the people every once in a while to see if they really did know them. Not only the children, who were always being heard for something, but everyone in the parish, both young and old, had to be heard. Every farmer in Lönneberga took a turn holding the hearing at his farm, and even if the actual hearing wasn't much fun, the feast afterwards always was. Anybody who lived in the parish could come, including the old folk from the poorhouse. Everyone who could possibly hobble always did come, for when there was a catechism hearing you could eat until you burst, and everyone enjoyed that.

One day in November, there was a catechism hearing at Katthult and that cheered everyone up, especially Lina, for she liked catechism hearings.

'What I don't like is all the questions,' she said, 'sometimes I hardly know what to answer.'

And it was true; Lina didn't know much about Bible stories. The parson was aware of that, and he gave her very easy questions for he was a kind man.

Now he had preached often about the Garden of Eden and Adam and Eve, the first people on earth. He thought that everyone must know the story by now, including Lina, so when it was her turn to be heard he asked in a friendly way, 'Now, Lina, what were the names of our first ancestors?'

'Thor and Freya,' said Lina promptly, and Emil's mother blushed with shame because of Lina's stupid answer. You see, Thor and Freya were two ancient Swedish gods whom the people in Småland worshipped long ago in heathen times, thousands of years before they'd ever heard of the Bible.

'You are a heathen and you always will be,' said Emil's mother to Lina afterwards.

But Lina answered back, 'Everything is so jumbled up, how am I expected to know who comes before who?'

But the parson was kind during the hearing. He passed over Lina's stupid answer and went straight on to tell how God had created the world and all the men who lived in it and how remarkable this creation was.

'You, too, Lina, are a real miracle,' the parson assured her, and he asked whether she had ever thought about it and whether she didn't think what a remarkable thing it was that God had created her.

Lina said she did think so, and then she added, 'It wasn't so remarkable to make *me*, but I think that all those curls and squirls in my ears must have been very difficult to make.'

Emil's mother blushed again, for she felt that the whole of Katthult was disgraced by Lina's stupid answers. It didn't improve matters when a ringing laugh came from the corner where Emil was. Poor Emil's mother, for you weren't supposed to laugh at catechism meetings. She sat there feeling ashamed and couldn't relax until the hearing was over and they could start the feasting.

Emil's mother had made all the good things that she always made for her parties, although Emil's father tried to put his foot down.

'The Bible stories and the catechism are supposed to be the important things, not meat-balls and cheesecakes, as you seem to think.'

'There's a time for everything,' Emil's mother said sagely. 'There's a time for the catechism, and there's a time for cheesecake.'

Yes, indeed, there was a time for cheesecake, and everyone at the catechism hearing at Katthult ate and enjoyed themselves. Emil also stuffed himself full of cheesecake covered with syrup and cream.

Then as soon as he had finished, his mother said, 'Emil, be a nice boy and go and lock up the hens.'

The hens scratched about outside all day long, but at night they had to be shut up because of the hungry fox that came sneaking round. It was almost dark and it was raining, but Emil was glad to get away from the stuffy room and the chatter and the cheesecake for a while. Most of the hens were

already sitting on their
perches in the hen house.
Only Lame Lotta and a
couple of other hens were
still scratching about outside in the rain, so Emil
shooed them in and fas-
tened the door. Now the
fox could come if he liked.
The pigsty was next to the

hen house so Emil looked in on Piggy-Beast for a
moment and promised him some titbits from the
evening's party.

'They always leave lots on their plates when
they're full up, the greedy pigs,' said Emil, and
Piggy-Beast grunted in agreement. 'I'll come back
later on.' Then he fastened the door of the pigsty.

Beyond the pigsty was the privy, that's what it
was called in those days. That's not a rude word, but
the privy at Katthult had an even more polite name.
It was called the Trisse hut because a farmhand

called Trisse had built the little necessary house a long time ago in Emil's grandfather's day.

Emil had fastened the hen-house door and he'd fastened the pigsty door and now, just to do the thing properly, he fastened the door of the Trisse hut, which was thoughtless of him. He should have realized that if the door was unfastened on the outside, there must have been someone inside. But Emil didn't stop to think. In no time he had fastened the door and danced off, singing loudly as he went, 'I've fastened here, I've fastened there, and now I've fastened everywhere!'

His father, who was in the Trisse hut, heard the cheerful song and foresaw the worst. He jumped up and tried the door. Sure enough, it was shut tight, and Emil's father bawled, 'EMIL!'

But Emil was already too far away and singing his song, 'I've fastened here—' so heartily that he couldn't hear a thing.

Poor Emil's father, he was so furious that he almost choked. This was absolutely awful, and how on earth was he going to get out? He hammered wildly on the door. He thumped and beat, but what was the use? Then he began to kick instead. He kicked the door until his toes curled under, but it held firm, for Trisse had done a first-rate job when he made that good solid door. Emil's father got wilder and wilder. He clawed frantically in his pockets for his clasp knife as he was sure he would be able to carve a hole big enough to stick the knife tip through and poke open the door, but the clasp knife was in the pocket of his work clothes and today he was wearing his Sunday best. For quite a while after that Emil's father stood there and hissed with fury. No, he didn't swear, because he was a churchwarden. But he hissed a lot about Emil and that wretched Trisse who hadn't made a proper window in the Trisse hut but only a narrow little opening high above the door. Emil's father glared at the window, which was far too small, and then he gave the door a couple more kicks. He ground his teeth in fury as he waited bloodthirstily for someone to come.

It's going to be just too bad for the first person who comes, because I'm going to murder him, he thought. This was really very unfair and not at all nice of Emil's father, but you must understand that he was very angry.

Darkness fell on the Trisse hut. Emil's father waited and waited, but no one came. He heard the rain drumming on the roof and it depressed him. He seethed and fumed. Here he was sitting all by himself in the darkness while everyone else was inside the brightly lit house having a good time and feasting at his expense. He wasn't going to stand for it any longer, he had to get out. Out! Even if it had to be through the opening.

'Now I'm mad,' he said aloud and stood up.

There was a box full of old newspapers in the Trisse hut. He tipped it on end, and then he stood on top of it. He found it was just the right height— so far so good. He pulled out the little window frame without any difficulty, and stuck his head through the hole and peered round for any sign of help.

There was no sign whatsoever, but the rain pelted down on the back of his neck and a lot of it ran down under his shirt collar and that's one of the worst places to have rain running down. But nothing could stop Emil's father now. He was going to get out even if there was a cloud burst pouring down on him.

With great difficulty he got his arms and shoulders through the hole, and then he wriggled up bit by bit.

You can do anything when you're really mad, he said to himself. But just then he came to a full stop, an absolute full stop. He struggled until he was blue in the face. He wildly kicked and swung his arms and legs, but all he managed to do was knock over the box; then he was hanging there without any foothold and unable to move either forwards or backwards, poor man!

What does a churchwarden do when his top half is hanging out in the pouring rain and his bottom half is dangling inside the privy? Does he

shout for help? No, he doesn't. No, because he knows the people of Lönneberga. He knows that if this spreads round the parish, the laughter will never stop while there's a living soul left in Lönneberga and the whole of Småland. Shout for help is what he *doesn't* do.

Meanwhile, Emil, who had returned to the party feeling pleased with himself, was doing his best to keep little Ida amused. She thought the catechism hearing was very boring, so he took her out into the passage and they had a lot of fun trying on over-shoes. There were long rows of them, large and small, and little Ida squealed with delight when Emil strode about in the parson's overshoes and said 'consequently' and 'what is more', just like the parson. In the end, the overshoes were scattered about all over the passage and Emil, tidy boy that he was, collected them all up in a heap in the middle of the floor. They made a small mountain.

Then he suddenly remembered that he had promised Piggy-Beast some leftovers from the feast. He went into the kitchen and scraped some of the leftovers into a dish. Carrying it in one hand and the farmyard lantern in the other, he went out into the rainy night to cheer up his little pig.

And then—Oh, I tremble when I think about it!—He saw his father. And his father saw him. Oh my goodness me!

'Go—and get—Alfred,' hissed his father, 'and tell him to bring a couple of pounds of dynamite because this Trisse hut is going to be flattened to the ground.'

Emil ran off and came back with Alfred. He didn't bring any dynamite—Emil's father hadn't really meant him to—but he did bring a saw because that was the only way to get Emil's father free.

While Alfred sawed, Emil stood perched on a ladder nervously holding an umbrella over his poor father to keep the rain off him. I can assure you that Emil didn't enjoy himself very much on that ladder, because his father spent the whole time hissing at him and telling him what he was going to do to him as soon as he was freed. He wasn't at all grateful to Emil for being so thoughtful in bringing the umbrella, either. What use was it, he grumbled, when he was already wet through to the skin and was going to catch cold anyway, followed by pneumonia, as sure as fate.

But Emil said, 'No, you won't catch a cold, for the main thing is to keep your feet dry.'

Alfred agreed with him. 'That's right, the main thing is to keep your feet dry.'

Emil's father could not deny that his feet were

dry, but he refused to be cheered up, and Emil dreaded the moment when his father should be freed.

The sawdust flew from Alfred's saw and Emil waited tensely. Then the moment came. Alfred sawed through the last inch of wood, Emil's father crashed to the ground, and Emil dropped the umbrella and bolted to the tool shed. He slipped inside with a second to spare and locked it in his father's face. It was lucky for Emil that his father had got tired of hammering on locked doors; he only hissed some threats at him and then went away. The important thing now was to be seen again at the feast. All he needed to do was to sneak quietly into the bedroom and put a dry shirt and jacket on his top half.

'Where have you been all this time?' asked Emil's mother in an unusually cross voice.

'I'll tell you about that later,' mumbled Emil's father.

And so the catechism hearing came to an end.

The parson struck up the usual hymn and all the people of Lönneberga joined in vigorously, each in his own key.

'Now the day is over, night is drawing nigh,' they sang. It was the time to make their way home in the November gloom. But when they went out into the passage to put on their coats, the first thing they saw by the weak light of the paraffin lamp was the mountain of overshoes in the middle of the floor.

'Only Emil could have done such an awful thing,' said the people of Lönneberga.

So they all had to sit down, the parson and his wife and everybody, and try on overshoes for two hours, and after that they all said goodbye rather sourly and went out into the rain.

They couldn't say goodbye to Emil, because he was sitting in the tool shed carving his one hundred and eighty-fourth wooden man.

*Saturday, the eighteenth of December, when Emil
did such a noble deed that the whole of Lönneberga
was proud of him and all his past tricks were forgiven
and forgotten.*

It was getting near Christmas. One evening everyone at Katthult was sitting in the kitchen busy at his own task. Emil's mother was treading the spinning-wheel, Emil's father was mending shoes, Lina was carding wool, Alfred and Emil were carving teeth for hay rakes, and little Ida was enjoying herself playing a children's finger game which interrupted Lina's work.

'You see, I have to do it to someone who's ticklish,' said little Ida, and Lina was the ideal person.

Ida walked her fingers slowly up Lina's dress, reciting this little rhyme:

> *Father mine and mother mine,*
> *Give me a little flour and salt,*
> *For I must kill my Christmas pig*
> *And when I kill him, he screams!*

When Ida came to 'screams', she poked Lina with her finger and sure enough, every single time, Lina screamed and laughed to Ida's great delight.

Emil's father was listening to the rhyme about 'kill my Christmas pig', and it must have started him thinking, because suddenly he said something awful.

'Yes, it's nearly Christmas, so it's about time for you to kill your pig, Emil.'

Emil dropped his knife and stared at his father.

'No one's going to kill Piggy-Beast,' he said, 'he's *my* pig, the one you gave me for taking the pledge. Don't you remember?'

Of course Emil's father remembered, but he said that no one in the whole of Småland had ever heard of a pet pig, and Emil was enough of a farmer to know that pigs had to be slaughtered when they were fat enough, because that was the only reason for keeping them.

'You ought to know that,' said Emil's father.

Yes, Emil knew it all right, and at first he couldn't think of an answer, but then he had a sudden idea.

'I'm enough of a farmer to know that lots of pigs are kept alive so that they can grow up to be boars, and I'd thought of that for Piggy-Beast.'

Emil knew what a boar was, but in case you don't know, I'll tell you that it is a pig who will become the father of lots of litters of little pigs, and Emil, being

151

a clever boy, had thought that to be a boar would be the salvation of Piggy-Beast.

He explained that his father would easily be able to find a sow for Piggy-Beast, and then Piggy-Beast and the sow would have masses of little piglets.

'That sounds all right,' said Emil's father, 'but it will be a poor sort of Christmas here at Katthult. No ham or sausages or blood puddings or anything.'

Give me a little flour and salt,
For I must make my good blood pudding,

sang little Ida, but Emil snapped at her, 'Shut up about making pudding.'

For he knew perfectly well that you need to have pig's blood, as well as flour and salt, to make blood puddings. But not Piggy-Beast's blood. Unless it was over Emil's dead body!

There was silence in the kitchen for some time. An unhappy silence. But suddenly Alfred swore. He had cut his thumb with his sharp knife, and the blood was pouring from it.

'Swearing isn't going to make it any better,' said Emil's father, sternly, 'and I won't have swear words in my house.'

Emil's mother fetched a clean piece of cloth and bandaged Alfred's thumb. Then he continued carving teeth for the hay rakes, as this was a job that had to be done in the winter. All the rakes had to be checked over and new teeth fitted where necessary so that the rake would be ready for spring.

'As I said, it's going to be a poor Christmas here at Katthult,' said Emil's father, gazing gloomily at the wall.

Emil couldn't go to sleep for a long time that night, and next morning he broke open his piggy bank and put thirty-five kronor in his pocket. Then he harnessed Lukas to an old sledge and drove to Bastefall where they had lots of pigs, and he came home with a fine fat pig which he put in the pigsty with Piggy-Beast. Then he went to see his father.

'Now there are two pigs in the pigsty,' he said. 'Go on and do your slaughtering, but I'm warning you, don't make a mistake.'

Emil was in a great rage, one of those rages that sometimes came over him, and he didn't care if he *was* talking to his father. Buying Piggy-Beast's life by having another poor pig killed in his place made him feel awful, but there was no other way to stop his father, because he simply didn't understand about pet pigs.

Emil didn't go to the pigsty for two days; he let Lina feed the pigs. On the morning of the third day he woke up when it was still pitch dark and heard a pig screaming for dear life. It was a high, piercing scream—then suddenly there was silence.

Emil blew on the frosted windowpane to make a peephole and looked out. He saw a lantern shining down by the pigsty and dark shadows moving about. Lina stood there stirring the blood that poured out of the pig. Later Alfred and Emil's father would scald the pig and shave it and cut it up; then Krösa-Maja and Lina would stand in the wash-house and clean it and that would be the end of the Bastefall pig that Emil had bought.

'When I kill him he screams,' muttered Emil, sliding back under the bedclothes and crying for a long time.

But man is made to forget and so did Emil. Early in the afternoon he sat for a while on the pigsty wall scratching Piggy-Beast's back and then he said thoughtfully, 'Anyway, you're alive and he isn't, Piggy-Beast. Fates are different in this world.'

Then he decided to forget all about the Bastefall pig. Next day, Krösa-Maja and Lina sat in the kitchen cutting up pork as fast as they could; Emil's mother stirred sausage meat and cooked blood puddings and cleaned the Christmas ham and put it in brine. Lina was singing, 'Cold, cold weather is blowing from the sea,' and Krösa-Maja was telling the story about a ghost in the graveyard that had no head. Emil enjoyed all this and thought no more about the Bastefall pig. He kept thinking that

Christmas would soon come and how nice it would be when it finally began to snow properly.

'Snow will come in buckets,' said little Ida, for that's what they say in Småland when it snows a lot.

And snow it did. It began as soon as it got dark, getting heavier and heavier, and the snow whirled down so that you could hardly see the farmyard when you looked through the window.

'There's going to be a real blizzard,' said Krösa-Maja. 'How am I going to get home?'

'You'll have to stay the night here,' said Emil's mother. 'You can sleep on the kitchen sofa with Lina.'

'All right, but you must lie as still as a dead pig,' said Lina, 'because you know how ticklish I am.'

After supper, Alfred complained about his thumb. He said it was hurting a lot, so Emil's mother unwound the bandage to see how it was healing.

She didn't like the look of it at all. Ugh! It was horrible. It was sore and red and swollen, and from

Alfred's wrists there were red streaks running a little way up his arm.

Krösa-Maja's eyes began to gleam.

'Blood poisoning,' she said, 'that's a very serious thing.'

Emil's mother fetched the bottle of medicine and put a poultice on Alfred's hand and forearm.

'If it's not better by morning, you'd better go to the doctor in Mariannelund,' she said.

That night all over Småland the snowstorm raged worse than anyone could remember ever having seen before. And when they woke up in the morning at Katthult the whole farmyard was covered in one big soft white snowdrift. The storm continued to rage; it snowed and blew so hard that you could barely put your nose outside, and the wind whistled down the chimney—wheee! No one had ever seen the like of it.

'Alfred'll have to shovel snow all day,' said Lina, 'though he might as well not bother as it won't do any good.'

Alfred didn't shovel any snow that day. When

they all sat down to breakfast his place at the kitchen table was empty, and there was no sign of him. Emil was worried. He put on his cap and his thick winter coat and went out. He picked up the snow shovel by the kitchen door and quickly cleared a path to the farmhand's hut next to the tool shed. Lina watched him through the kitchen window and nodded approvingly.

'How clever of Emil to think of clearing a path to the tool shed now. Then he'll be all ready for when he has to go there.'

Silly Lina, she didn't realize that Emil was going to see Alfred.

It felt cold in the hut when Emil stepped inside. Alfred hadn't lit the stove. He lay on his bed and wouldn't get up. He didn't want any food either. He wasn't hungry, he said. That made Emil even more worried. If Alfred wasn't hungry, there was something seriously wrong with him.

Emil put some wood on the stove and lit it, then he went to fetch his mother.

She came and so did all the others, Emil's father and Lina and Krösa-Maja and little Ida, for now they were all worried about Alfred.

Poor Alfred, he just lay there with his eyes closed. He was as hot as a chimney and yet he was shivering. The red streaks, which had crept right up to his armpits, looked terrible.

Krösa-Maja nodded her head knowingly, 'When those streaks reach the heart, that's the end, he'll die.'

'Be quiet,' said Emil's mother, but it wasn't so easy to silence Krösa-Maja. She knew of at least half a dozen people in Lönneberga parish alone who had died of blood poisoning, and she insisted on counting them all upon her fingers, one by one.

'But that doesn't mean that we must give up hope for Alfred,' she said.

She thought it might help if they took a lock of his hair and a piece of his shirt and buried them at midnight to the north of the house and then said a really good charm; she knew one, she said. 'Fie, fie, may what comes from the devil go back to the devil. Fie, fie!'

But Emil's father said that the swear word Alfred had said when he cut his thumb was quite enough and if anything was to be buried to the north of the house at midnight in this weather, Krösa-Maja could do it herself.

Krösa-Maja shook her head gloomily. 'Nature will take its toll, oh dear me, yes.'

Emil was furious. 'What sort of old wives' talk is that? Alfred will soon be better, do you understand?'

Then Krösa-Maja changed her tone and said, 'Yes, of course, Emil my boy, of course he'll get better.' And just to be on the safe side, she patted Alfred as he lay there, and added loudly, 'Of course you'll get better, Alfred, I'm sure you will.'

Then she looked at the door and muttered to herself, 'But I don't know how they're going to get the coffin through that narrow door!'

Emil heard her and began to cry. He tugged anxiously at his father's coat.

'We must take Alfred to the doctor at Mariannelund like Mamma said.'

Emil's father and mother looked at each other. They knew it was going to be impossible to get to Mariannelund that day. Yes, it was quite hopeless, but it was difficult to bluntly tell Emil when he stood there looking so upset. Really, Emil's father and mother wanted to help Alfred in any way they could, but they just didn't know what they could do, and so they didn't know what to say to Emil.

Emil's father slouched away from the hut without saying anything, but Emil didn't give up. He followed his father round, crying and pleading and shouting and threatening, and, just think, his father didn't get cross, but simply answered quietly, 'We can't do anything, Emil. You know we can't.'

Lina sat in the kitchen, crying her eyes out and saying, 'And there was me thinking we'd get married in the spring. It's goodbye to all that. It's all over with Alfred and here am I left with four sheets and a whole dozen towels. That's a fine state of affairs.'

At last Emil knew it was true. There was nothing they could do. He went back to the hut and sat with Alfred all day. It was the longest day in his life. Alfred lay with his eyes shut, but once in a while he opened them and every time he said, 'Ah, there you are, Emil.'

As Emil watched the snow whirling down outside the window, his hatred for the snow was so intense and fiery that it ought to have been able to melt every snowflake in Lönneberga and the whole of Småland. But it didn't. Instead, the snow came down so heavily that he thought the whole world was going to perish in it.

Winter days are short, even if they seem long for people who are sitting and waiting like Emil was. It was getting dusk and soon it would be dark.

'Ah, there you are, Emil,' said Alfred again, but it was more difficult for him to get the words out now.

Emil's mother brought out some meat broth and made Emil drink it. She tried to get Alfred to have some, too, but he didn't want any. Emil's mother just sighed and went away.

Quite late in the evening Lina came to say it was Emil's bedtime. He must know it was late.

'I'm going to sleep on the floor next to Alfred,' said Emil. And that's what he did.

He scouted round for an old mattress and a heavy blanket. That was all he needed to sleep on. But he couldn't sleep. He could only lie awake and watch the fire dying in the stove as he listened to Alfred's alarm clock ticking and Alfred's rapid breathing and the moans he made from time to time. He dozed now and then, but every so often he woke up with a sudden start and felt guilty. As the night went by, he felt more and more how wrong it all was and how it would soon be too late, too late for ever, to do anything about it.

At four o'clock in the morning Emil made up his mind what he must do. He must take Alfred to the doctor at Mariannelund even if both he and Alfred died in the attempt.

You're not going to just lie in your bed and die, Alfred. I'm not going to let you. He didn't say it aloud, he only thought it to himself, but he meant it. Emil started to make preparations at once. He had to be gone before anyone woke up and tried to stop him. He had an hour before Lina got up to milk the cows, and he had to get everything done within that hour.

No one will ever know how hard Emil worked. The sledge had to be taken out of the cart shed, Lukas had to be taken out of his stall and harnessed, and Alfred had to be taken out of bed and put into the sledge—and that was the hardest of all. Poor Alfred, he staggered and leaned heavily on Emil, and when he finally managed to reach the sledge, he just slumped over into the sheepskin rugs and lay there as if he were already dead. Emil tucked the rugs round Alfred so that only his nose was visible, then he got into the driver's seat and shook the reins, shouting 'Gee-up' to Lukas. But Lukas turned round and looked with disbelief at Emil. Didn't

Emil understand that it was absolutely foolish to go out in all this snow?

'I'm the one who gives the orders now, Lukas, but on the road it'll be up to you.'

A light went on in the kitchen, which meant that Lina was awake. They were getting under way just in time; Emil and horse and sledge swished out of the Katthult gate down the road through the wind and the snow.

Ugh, what horrible weather it was! The snow got in Emil's ears and lay thickly on his eyes so that he couldn't see anything—and he needed to see the road. He wiped his mitten across his face, but he still couldn't see the road, although there were two coach lamps on the sledge. There was no road. There was only snow. But Lukas had been to Mariannelund many times and perhaps deep down in his horse's memory he knew where the road was. He was just the right sort of horse to have with you in the snow. Somehow or other he continued to pull the sledge through the drifts. It was a slow job, and

there was a great jolt every time the sledge stuck firmly. But they moved forward little by little. Again and again Emil had to get off the sledge and shovel the snow. He was as strong as a young ox, and he shovelled so much snow that night that he never forgot it.

'You find you're very strong when you *have* to be,' he explained to Lukas.

And indeed Emil was strong. All went well for the first mile or so, but then it got difficult. Yes, it turned into a real nightmare for Emil. He was tired now, the shovel felt so heavy and he couldn't get a really good swing with it any longer. He was freezing, he had snow in his boots and pins and needles in his toes. His fingers ached with cold and so did his ears, in spite of the woollen scarf he had tied over his cap to keep his ears from being blown off. Altogether, it was miserable, and Emil's spirits sank lower and lower. Suppose his father had been right when he said, 'We can't do anything, Emil. You know we can't.'

Lukas also began to slow down. It became more and more difficult for the horse to free the sledge when it got stuck, and at last what Emil had been afraid of all along happened. The sledge suddenly sank, and Emil realized that they were in the ditch.

Yes, they were in the ditch and there they stayed. Lukas pulled and tugged with all his might and Emil pushed until his nose bled, but it made no difference. The sledge would not budge.

Then Emil went into a wild rage because of the snow and the sledge and the ditch and the frustration of it all. Something seemed to snap inside him and he let out a great yell of desperation. Lukas was startled and perhaps Alfred was too; but he showed no signs of life. Emil was suddenly frightened and stopped in mid yell.

'Are you still alive, Alfred?' he asked nervously.

'No. I think I am dead now,' said Alfred in a strange, croaking, horrible voice. Then all the fury went out of Emil, and he felt a great sorrow. Although Alfred lay there in the sledge, Emil was all alone and had no one to help him. He just didn't know what to do. He felt like lying down in the snow and sleeping and sleeping and forgetting all about everything.

But not far from the road was a farm; Emil called it the Pancake Place because of two small, chubby children who had once stood by the gate eating pancakes as Emil went by. Suddenly, he saw a light in the barn.

'I'm going to fetch help, Alfred,' he said, but Alfred didn't answer. He ploughed through the deep drifts and when he stepped through the barn door he looked more like a snowman than anything else.

The Pancake farmer himself was in the barn, and he was very surprised to see the Katthult boy standing in the doorway with his nose bleeding and tears in his eyes. Emil was crying now, he couldn't help it and, worse still, he knew the Pancake farmer wouldn't want to go out into the snow. The Pancake farmer wasn't at all pleased about it, but he couldn't very well say no; so he brought out a horse and a rope and a hook and pulled the sledge out of the ditch, but he was grumbling all the time.

If the Pancake farmer had had any decency he would have tried to help Emil to get through to Mariannelund, but he didn't. Emil and Lukas were left to continue toiling desperately through the snowdrifts as best they could. But they couldn't go on for much longer. They both struggled as hard as they could, but they were so tired that

they moved forward very slowly. Finally, Emil had to give up. He could do no more, he couldn't even lift the snow shovel.

'I can't go on any longer, Alfred,' he said and started to cry. It was only about a mile to Mariannelund, and it was heart-breaking to have to give up when they were so near.

There was no sound from Alfred. He was probably dead. Lukas stood with bowed head as if he were ashamed of himself, but he couldn't go on any longer, either.

Emil climbed into the driving seat and sat there. He cried quietly, the snow fell on him, and he didn't move. It was all over now, it could continue to snow as much as it liked, and he didn't care any more.

He couldn't keep his eyes open; he wanted to sleep. In fact, all he wanted to do was to sit in the driver's seat and let the snow cover him up.

But there wasn't any snow, and there wasn't any winter. He drifted off to sleep, and it was summer, and he and Alfred were swimming in the lake at Katthult. Alfred wanted to teach Emil to swim. Silly Alfred, didn't he know that Emil knew how to swim already? Alfred himself had taught him several years ago, had he forgotten? Emil had to show him how well he could swim, so they swam and swam and swam together, further out into the lake. It was lovely in the water, and Emil said, 'Just you and me, Alfred,' and he waited for Alfred to answer as he always did, 'That's right, Emil, just you and me.' Instead he heard the sound of sleigh bells and that was all wrong. There aren't supposed to be sleigh bells when you are swimming.

Emil forced himself awake and opened his eyes. *Then he saw the snowplough.* A snowplough was coming through the blizzard, yes, it was a snowplough from Mariannelund. And the man driving it thought he was seeing a ghost and not a little boy from Katthult completely covered with snow.

'Is the road cleared all the way to Mariannelund?' asked Emil, excitedly.

'Yes, if you hurry,' answered the driver. 'In half an hour it'll be as bad as ever again.'

But half an hour was enough time for Emil.

The doctor's waiting room was full of people. The doctor had just put his head round the door of his operating room to see who was next, when all the people in the waiting room nearly jumped out of their seats, because Emil rushed in, shouting, 'Alfred's dying in the sledge outside!'

The doctor didn't waste time. He got two of the patients in the waiting room to carry Alfred inside and lay him on the operating table.

He took one look at Alfred, and then he called out, 'Go home, all of you, I've got work to do.'

Emil had thought that Alfred would get better the moment he arrived at the doctor's, but when he saw the doctor shaking his head rather like Krösa-Maja had done, he was scared. Suppose it was too late after all, suppose Alfred couldn't be cured? He felt sick with fear, and choking with tears he grabbed the doctor and screamed at him, 'I'll give you my horse if you make him better. And my pig, if only you make him better. Do you think you can?'

The doctor looked at Emil solemnly. 'I'll do what I can, but I'm not making any promises.'

Alfred was lying there showing no signs of life, but all at once he opened his eyes and looked at Emil vaguely.

'There you are, Emil,' he said.

'Yes, Emil's here, but it's better if he goes out now for a little while, because I've got to operate, Alfred.'

You could tell by Alfred's eyes that he was frightened. He wasn't used to doctors and the things they did.

'I think he's a bit afraid,' said Emil. 'It might be best if I stay here.'

The doctor nodded. 'If you could stand up to that journey, you can stand up to this.'

Emil held Alfred's good hand firmly while the

doctor cut into the other one. Alfred didn't make a sound. He neither screamed nor cried, although Emil cried a little, but quietly to himself so that no one noticed.

Emil didn't return home with Alfred until the day before Christmas Eve. Then the whole of Lönneberga learned about his noble deed, and everyone felt very proud of him.

They all said, 'I've always liked that Katthult boy. I don't know why people are always grumbling about him. All boys get into mischief sometimes.'

Emil had brought back a letter from the doctor for his father and mother, and in it the doctor had written: 'You have a boy you can be proud of.' Emil's mother wrote in the blue exercise book: 'Dear Lord, how soothing to my poor mother's heart. The times I've been in despair about Emil. But now I am going to see that everyone in the parish hears about this, and that's for certain.'

But what a time they had at Katthult on the awful morning when they discovered that Emil and

Alfred had disappeared. Emil's father was in such a state that he got a pain in his stomach and had to go to bed. He thought he would never see Emil alive again. Later, a message arrived from Mariannelund that put his mind at ease, but he still had a stomach ache when Emil came back and rushed into the bedroom to tell his father he was home again.

Emil's father's eyes glistened when he looked at Emil.

'You're a good boy, Emil,' he said, and Emil was so pleased that his heart danced inside him. This was one of the days when he did like his father.

Emil's mother stood there glowing with pride, 'Yes, he's a fine lad, our Emil,' she said, and patted his shaggy head.

Emil's father lay with a warm saucepan lid on his stomach, because it was so soothing, but now it had cooled and needed warming up again.

'I'll do it,' shouted Emil eagerly. 'I'm good at nursing now.'

Emil's father nodded approvingly.

'And *you* can get me a glass of juice,' he said to Emil's mother.

This was an ideal arrangement. All he had to do was lie in bed and be waited on by everybody.

But Emil's mother had other things to do, so it was a little while before she could get the juice ready. Then, just as she was finally pouring it out she heard a great bellow coming from the bedroom. It was Emil's father. As Emil's mother rushed in, the saucepan lid came rolling straight at her. She dodged it quickly, but in her fright she spilt the juice, and it splashed on to the saucepan lid where it sizzled fiercely.

'Good gracious! How hot did you make the lid?' she asked Emil, who stood looking bewildered.

'About as hot as an iron,' said Emil.

Apparently Emil's father had fallen asleep while Emil was in the kitchen heating the saucepan lid. When Emil returned he found his father sleeping peacefully and didn't want to wake him up; so he slid the lid carefully in beneath the covers and laid it on his father's stomach. Yes, it was bad luck that the lid was too hot.

Emil's mother did what she could to calm him.

'There now, there now, I'm just bringing the liniment,' she said.

But Emil's father got up. He said he didn't think he'd better stay in bed any longer now that Emil was home, and besides he wanted to go and say 'hello' to Alfred.

Alfred sat in the kitchen, looking very pale with his arm still in a sling, but he was happy and cheerful, and Lina joyously hovered round him. She and Krösa-Maja were busy scouring the copper bowls and pots and pans which had to be all bright and shining for Christmas. But Lina couldn't keep still. She snuggled near Alfred with her cleaning rag in one hand and the cheesecake mould in the other and behaved as if she had unexpectedly found a gold nugget in her kitchen. Little Ida couldn't take her eyes off Alfred either. She looked at him gravely, trying to make up her mind if it was the same old Alfred who had come home.

Krösa-Maja had one of her greatest moments; she talked about blood poisoning until she frothed at the mouth. She said that Alfred should consider himself lucky that things had turned out as they did.

'But you must be very careful, for blood poisoning is such a long serious business that you're ill long after you've got better.'

They had a great time at Katthult that evening. Emil's mother brought out the new oatmeal sausages. They had a real oatmeal sausage feast, sitting happily all together in the Christmassy kitchen, Emil and his father and mother and little Ida and Alfred and Lina and Krösa-Maja. Yes, it was just like Christmas Eve, with candles on the table and everything. And the oatmeal sausages were so delicious, fried crisp and brown, and everyone ate them with fresh whortleberries. Alfred ate most of all, though it was a little tricky for him with only one hand.

Lina looked lovingly at him and suddenly came up with a bright idea, 'Well, Alfred, now that you haven't got blood poisoning, we can get married in the spring, can't we?'

Alfred got such a fright that he spilt whortle berries all over his trousers.

'I'm not promising anything,' he said. 'I've still got another thumb. Who's to say that I won't get blood poisoning in that one, too?'

'If you do that,' said Emil, 'I'll bury you to the north of the house and that's for sure, because I'm not going to take you to Mariannelund again.'

Krösa-Maja glared at Emil.

'All you do is make fun of everything,' she said in a hurt voice.

While they were all sitting there in the Christmassy candlelight, Emil's mother took the doctor's letter out of her apron pocket and read out loud what he had written about Emil. She decided it wouldn't do any harm if everyone heard it. After she finished reading, everyone was silent. They were silent because the letter was so full of long fine words.

Finally, little Ida said, 'That was about you, Emil.'

Emil was embarrassed and didn't know what to do with himself. They were all looking at him and he felt uncomfortable, so he stared stubbornly out of the window. But that didn't make him feel much better, because he noticed it was snowing again, and he knew who would have to get up early in the morning and shovel.

He attacked the sausages again, but he ate with downcast eyes and only glanced up quickly to see if they were still looking at him.

His mother was, at any rate. She couldn't take her eyes off her beloved boy. He looked so sweet as he sat there with his rosy cheeks and his curly fair hair and his innocent blue eyes. He was just like a little Christmas angel; besides, she had the doctor's word that she could be proud of him.

'It's funny,' said Emil's mother, 'sometimes when I

look at Emil I have a feeling that he is going to be very important some day.'

Emil's father looked doubtful.

'Important in what way?' he asked.

'How should I know? President of the local council perhaps—or anything.'

Lina guffawed.

'You can't have a president of the local council who *plays tricks*,' she said.

Emil's mother looked at her sternly, but didn't say anything, she only passed the dish of sausages round with sharp, angry jerks.

Emil helped himself, and while he slowly poured whortleberry juice over the sausages he began to wonder about what his mother had said. Just think, suppose he really did become president of the local council when he grew up. That wasn't a bad idea; someone had to be president.

Then he began to wonder about what Lina had said. Supposing he became a president of the council who did play tricks, what sort of tricks would they be?

He poured milk into his glass and continued to think about it—president-of-the-local-council tricks would obviously have to be very special, you wouldn't be able to think those up in a flash. Just as he was going to take a drink of milk, he thought of a marvellous trick and burst out laughing so that the milk shot across the table and splurted on to his father.

Emil's father didn't say much, because after all he couldn't get very cross with someone the doctor had praised so highly and who had done such a noble deed. He merely wiped himself dry and said rather bitterly, 'We can see who's come home again.'

'Don't say things like that,' said Emil's mother reproachfully, and Emil's father said no more, but began to think about his son's future.

'I doubt if he will become president of the local council,' he said at last, 'but he might well turn out to be a good citizen. So long as he stays in good health and lives long enough and God wills it.'

Emil's mother nodded in agreement, 'Yes, if God wills it.'

'And if Emil wills it,' said little Ida.

Emil gave a little smile.

'That remains to be seen,' said Emil.

Then evening came and the night fell. Everyone went to bed and slept peacefully, and the snow fell down on the whole of Katthult and the whole of Lönneberga and the whole of Småland.

ASTRID LINDGREN

Astrid Lindgren was born in Vimmerby, Sweden in 1907. In the course of her life she wrote over 40 books for children, and has sold over 145 million copies worldwide. She once commented, 'I write to amuse the child within me, and can only hope that other children may have some fun that way too'.

Many of Astrid Lindgren's stories are based upon her memories of childhood and they are filled with lively and unconventional characters. Perhaps the best known is *Pippi Longstocking*, first published in Sweden in 1945. It was an immediate success, and was published in England in 1954.

Awards for Astrid Lindgren's writing include the prestigious Hans Christian Andersen Award and the International Book Award. In 1989 a theme park dedicated to her — Astrid Lindgren Varld — was opened in Vimmerby. She died in 2002 at the age of 94.